I0643312

George Burnett Barton

Literature in New South Wales

George Burnett Barton

Literature in New South Wales

ISBN/EAN: 9783337328016

Printed in Europe, USA, Canada, Australia, Japan

Cover: Foto ©Andreas Hilbeck / pixelio.de

More available books at **www.hansebooks.com**

Dedicated

TO

THE HONOURABLE

TERENCE AUBREY MURRAY,

PRESIDENT OF THE LEGISLATIVE COUNCIL,

AND

EXECUTIVE COMMISSIONER FOR THE PARIS EXHIBITION:

AT WHOSE REQUEST

THESE PAGES HAVE BEEN WRITTEN.

LITERATURE IN NEW SOUTH WALES.

To trace the growth of letters in this community, from the earliest period of our history to the present time, and to shew in what manner that growth has been influenced by the productions of the Mother Country, are the objects sought to be accomplished in these pages. With us, Literature requires to be considered in two aspects: first, as a native or indigenous product; and secondly, as a foreign or imported one. Too young to possess a " national literature" of our own, the consideration of foreign influence becomes an all-important one. With respect to the literary productions of the Colony, a detailed account of them will be found in subsequent pages. It seemed desirable to map out the whole field of intellectual energy, and, by adopting a critical as well as a chronological method, to ascertain the precise result of our labours. This would amount to a literary history of the Colony, and it was hoped that such a history would serve more than one useful purpose. It would enable the reader to form an exact idea of the progress, extent, and prospects of literary enterprise among us, more readily than could be done by means of any general statement; it would constitute a bibliographical account that might be practically useful, not only to those who are interested in our literature, but also to those who may hereafter be engaged in historical inquiries; it would serve to throw some light, from a new point of view, on our social history; and lastly, it would preserve the memory, and give some notion of the achievements, of men whose name could scarcely be expected to survive their generation. These were the expectations which induced the writer to enter upon such a task. The difficulties encountered in its performance were greater than would be easily believed, and must form the writer's excuse for whatever errors or omissions may be discovered. It is not irrelevant to state what these difficulties were.

In the first place, it has not proved an easy matter to procure the necessary material. No collection, in the interest of the public, has yet been made of the widely scattered mass of books and papers which constitute our literature. Every one knows how rapidly these things are apt to disappear. Newspapers and magazines are thrown aside as soon as they are read. Books too often share the same fate. Thus it happens that, in the course of a few years, it becomes almost a hopeless task to recover these neglected treasures. However absurd it may seem to say so, it is nevertheless true that there is already a field for literary antiquarianism among us, and more than one antiquarian is vigorously at work. The collection made by the late Mr. Justice Wise, imperfect as it is, amply demonstrates this truth. Without the assistance of that collection, the facts gathered together in this work could never have been obtained. Much of our periodical literature has vanished. Portions of it may be found in dusty corners of public libraries, and other portions in the hands of private collectors. Were they thrown together, we should possess ample means for estimating our progress in letters, as well as a valuable source of information on our past history. It is to be hoped that this will be accomplished before it becomes too late to attempt it. Such a collection has already been made in Victoria, where the importance of local publications, as materials for History, is fully felt.

In the second place, there is some difficulty in determining what works come within the limits of our literature. As regards publications by native authors, there is, of course, no difficulty ;

but in the case of authors not born within the Colony, the point is not always easy to determine. The number of books written about Australia, or on subjects connected with it, is very great. Some have been written by men who have spent their lives in it, others by men who have been only casual residents. The rule which has been acted on in these pages is, to exclude all works not written by men who have identified themselves with the Colony, or who have made it, in the common phrase, " their adopted country." An exception may be found here and there, when the interest of the subject warranted it. Observing this rule, it makes no difference whether a particular book was published in Sydney or in London. The place of publication is merely a matter of convenience, and in most cases it will be found that books not intended for strictly local circulation have been published in London. It must be recollected that there are two very strong reasons against publishing in Sydney. The first is, that the expense is nearly twice as great ; and the second, that no work published in the Colonies has any chance of finding a sale in London. Everything of importance that has issued from the local press has been included,—the only exception being where the work could not be found.

Looking at this catalogue of our performances, it will probably be considered that more has been done among us in the way of literature than might have been expected. We have not suffered ourselves to be discouraged by the difficulties in our path, and we have not neglected the few advantages we possess. In every department of letters we have produced something of more or less value—something to shew that original intellects have been at work. In more than one instance, there is evidence of undoubted genius to be found. It is natural that our energies should have sought a field rather in newspapers and other publications of the kind, than in more permanent forms. Newspapers are matters of commercial necessity, and consequently there is always a demand for them. Our list of these publications is a very lengthy one. During the last thirty years, there seems to have been a great amount of activity in this way, scarcely a year passing by without some new competitors for public favour. Many of these, no doubt, displayed but a moderate share of ability ; but on the other hand, there were many in whose pages may be found evidence of very striking talent. The present state of our periodical literature, it must be confessed, does not adequately represent the great advance made by this Colony in wealth and refinement. We have two daily papers, but their attention is necessarily devoted more to matters of business than anything else : nor is either distinguished by the splendour of the editorial intellect. We have several weekly newspapers, but they address themselves to particular sections, and none of them can be read for anything beyond the intelligence it supplies. We have no magazine ; the last died eight years ago, and there is little probability of another. We have one comic periodical, and that is the only publication that attempts to exist as a purely literary production.

Turning to other fields, we may say that the rough groundwork of a " national literature " has been laid. Poetry has been diligently cultivated, and, in some instances, not in vain. One or two volumes display the unmistakeable hand of genius. The splendid scenery of our native land has not remained unsung ; something distinctively Australian has resulted from its worship. In prose Fiction, more than one creditable effort has been made. The History of the Colony—in a great measure, of all Australia— has been exhaustively written. Our narratives of Exploration have been read with interest in circles far beyond our own firesides. Much has been done by us towards elucidating the great mystery of Australian geography, and the Chronicles that have been written on the subject possess a lasting value. Nor have we been inattentive to other problems that concern us. The dialects of the aboriginal tribes have, to some extent, been reduced to grammatical form. The importance of the subject is fully felt, and in a short time it may be hoped that many more sheaves will be gathered from the fields. In Ethnology we can point to a work that has been deservedly said to contain one of the most "interesting literary discoveries of the present age." In certain special fields, much useful work has been done. We have no reason to be ashamed of our efforts in Physical Science. Two or three useful Societies have been established for some years, and their members have not been idle. The Geology and Natural History of the country have long since been made known to the scientific world.

Considering the circumstances under which all this has been accomplished,—the difficulties in the way, and the slight inducement in the shape of either fame or reward,—we may perhaps claim to have done our duty. Seventy-eight years only have passed since the first fleet from England cast anchor in our harbour. During that period—a single life-time—we have civilized and fertilized a wilderness; explored unknown regions, bristling with dangers that defied alike ingenuity and valour; pushed our settlements across mountains deemed impenetrable, and rivers flooded with the rains of winter; built a city surpassed in beauty by no city on the earth,—filled it with the merchandise of the world, and thronged its harbour with trafficers from every port in Europe. And while we have thus achieved a degree of material prosperity unprecedented in history, we have achieved our political independence also. Let it be added, we have become a parent state, while yet in our own infancy. Victoria, Tasmania, Queensland, and New Zealand, are but offshoots from the tree which we have planted. Surely this was work enough for the hands and brains of one or two generations—enough, at any rate, to account for some degree of materialism in our social character. Yet with all these labours upon us, we have not neglected the higher interests of humanity. We have not wholly devoted ourselves to gold-digging and sheep-shearing, to the cares of the counting-house and the shop. The wealth we have earned has been devoted to noble purposes. The best results of civilization have been eagerly sought for and welcomed. Temples have been built for their habitation, though their architecture may be mean, and their worshippers but few.

In reviewing our periodical literature, a fact becomes apparent which is not, at first sight, easy to account for. It is this,—that the cleverest and most promising publications—those in which there has been a special recognition of literature—have invariably failed. A good weekly newspaper, in which something more than news and advertisements may be found, is generally a popular and successful publication. Several attempts have been made to establish one. Not one has succeeded. Again, few publications are more universally in request than magazines. Several attempts have been made to establish one. Not one has succeeded. Now, in neither of these cases, is the failure always to be ascribed to want of ability. In more than one instance, very great ability has been shewn. In what way then, is it to be accounted for ? The failure of these publications proves one of two things, if not both: (1) That there was not sufficient talent to render them worth supporting ; or (2) That there was no desire among the public generally to support them. Either one or other must be the reason why the most attractive portion of the newspaper press has always come to grief. A slight discussion of these points will tend to illustrate the present state of literature in this country.

It is well known that, to give sufficient attractiveness to publications basing their claims to support on their literary character, a large staff of competent writers is indispensable. One or two clever writers alone will not do. Amateur writers will not do. There must be a reliable "staff," as it is termed. Now it has rarely or never happened that such assistance could be procured in the Colony. We have rarely or never had among us a sufficient number of professed men of letters to carry on such undertakings. There has always been one or two, and there have sometimes been three or four. It was a natural result, therefore, that our high-class journalism should have fallen to the ground. After the issue of a few numbers, the editor and his assistants have apparently become exhausted, and subscribers have disappeared. We are no better off, in this respect, at the present time. A magazine could scarcely be produced with any reasonable chance of success, simply on this account. This, then, may be one reason for the poor character of our present journalism; but, at the same time, it would not be safe to assert that it is the sole reason. It could not be safely asserted that, if a sufficient number of writers could be obtained, any kind of publication, however ambitious, might be started with confidence. Why so? Is the community insensible to literature? Is it too small, or too poor, to support it? This is not the character of our community, and consequently another reason must be looked for. It will be found in the fact that it is prejudiced against local productions,—or, if not prejudiced, at least unwilling to support them.

The best evidence that can be furnished on this point is, the circulation of English periodicals throughout the Colony. If it were the case that the demand for these productions is very slight, we should then conclude that the community is either insensible to art altogether, or that it is too limited in its means to support it. But the case is not so. The demand for English periodicals is very great. The number imported every month is far larger than would be readily supposed. The *Cornhill* alone, for instance, has several hundred subscribers. *All the Year Round* and *Once a Week* are extremely popular. One bookseller sells a thousand volumes of *Good Words* every year. Another sells five hundred. *Punch* and the *Illustrated London News* are read by every one. The *London Journal*, the *Family Herald*, the *Englishwoman's Domestic Magazine*, and similar periodicals, may be said to circulate by cart-loads. To say, in the face of these facts, that there is no demand for popular literature among us, would be absurd. Contrasting the eagerness to obtain these publications with the fate of similar publications attempted in the Colony, there is only one conclusion to be drawn.

There are about a dozen booksellers and news-agents in Sydney who import English periodicals for subscribers. The writer having been furnished by them with their lists, the total number of copies received monthly, and the estimated value of the yearly subscription, are given here. The figures represent a very close approximation to the exact number of copies circulated monthly in the Colony. They are certainly within the mark. If a slight addition is made on account of chance sales, the reader will know pretty well what the total circulation amounts to ; and he will also be able to form his own conclusions as to the style of reading most in vogue. The circulation of different periodicals is no doubt influenced by their price. The subscription to *Blackwood*, for instance, is two guineas, while the subscription to the *Cornhill* is only eighteen shillings. It is necessary to point out that all weekly publications, excepting mere newspapers, reach us in monthly parts, or half-yearly volumes.

REVIEWS.	No. of Copies.	Value of Yearly Subscription.
		£ s.
Edinburgh ...	40	60 0
Quarterly ...	46	69 0
Westminster * ...	20	30 0
British Quarterly ...	7	10 10
North British	5	7 10
Dublin	5	7 10
MAGAZINES.		
Cornhill	425 ...	340 0
Argosy	110 ...	100 0
Blackwood	92 ...	160 15

* Mr. Fowler's statements in his *Southern Lights*, with respect to the circulation of English periodicals in the Colony are not confirmed by the figures given above. He says :— " The best patronised Review is the *Westminster*. The *Athenæum* circulates all over the " Colony. The *Examiner*, the *Spectator*, the *Leader*, the *Dispatch*, and *Lloyd's* are the " favourite journals." The three first-mentioned journals are hardly known.

	No. of Copies.	Value of Yearly Subscription.
		£ s.
Macmillan	68	54 8
Temple Bar	65	58 10
Fraser ...	43	75 5
Eclectic...	10	9 0
Bentley	5	10 10
All the Year round	335	234 5
Chambers' Journal	203	121 16
Once a Week ...	176	151 8
London Society	170	153 0
Punch	690	724 10
Fun	75	45 0
Athenæum ...	28	28 0
Art Journal ...	15	31 10
Saturday Review	134	281 8
Reader	62	62 0

MISCELLANIES.

				No. of Copies.		Value of Yearly Subscription.
Good Words ...	...	...	1,750		875 0
London Journal	...	...	1,500		750 0
Family Herald	...	...	...	900		450 0
Reynolds' Miscellany ...	...	...	500		250 0
Englishwoman's Domestic Magazine ..			360		324 0
Cassell's Family Paper	...	...	350		175 0
Bow Bells ...	...	...	280		140 0
Leisure Hour ...	...	...	200		100 0
Sunday at Home	...		100		50 0
Sunday Magazine	...		50		25 0

NEWSPAPERS.

		No. of Copies.		Value of Yearly Subscription.
Home News ...	...	1,500	...	1,050 0
Illustrated News	...	1,320	...	2,772 0
Lloyd's Weekly	...	500	...	125 0
Illustrated Times	...	240	...	240 0
Dispatch ...	...	130	...	65 0
Public Opinion	...	90	...	90 0
Bell's Life ...	...	70	...	147 0
Field ...	...	70	...	147 0
Totals	...	12,739		£10,600 15

What has been said respecting periodicals applies equally to books. The average value of books imported during the year is not less than £50,000. This may be taken to represent 100,000 volumes at least. Every work embraced in the term "popular literature," is sure to find its way out here. But there is no eagerness to welcome any local production, of any kind whatever. There is no instance, known to the writer, of any work published in Sydney having met with a large sale, or even a tolerably large sale. The probability is, that every case of publication, not by means of subscription, has involved a loss.

It is, of course, impossible to say how far these circumstances—the capacity of our writers and the temper of the public—influence each other. On the one hand, it might be said that, if there is a want of the necessary ability, it is owing to the indifference of the public; and on the other hand, it might be said that, if the public is indifferent, it is owing to the want of talent in the publications offered to them. Generally speaking, where there is a demand for any commodity, there is sure to be a supply. If there existed a general willingness to support local productions, and by that means to raise the standard of intelligence, such speculations would be profitable—periodicals would appear—talent would command a fair remuneration—and if it could not be found on the spot, it would be obtained elsewhere. It is clear that the community is not insensible to the attractions of literature. The fact is quite the reverse. All that can be said is, that it is insensible to the importance of encouraging local productions. A question may certainly be raised as to whether there is any importance at all in the matter. Looking at it in a commercial light, it may be said, " Why should local productions be encouraged, when foreign productions of a better quality may be had? If it is a case of boots and saddles, every one scouts the idea of a protective tariff; and why not with periodicals as with manufactures?" Something of this kind seems to be the prevalent feeling. Now if literature meant nothing more than books or magazines in themselves, the argument might be tolerably conclusive ; but it no more means that, than Religion means Calvin's Institutes or Jeremy Taylor's Sermons.

In a society animated by such feelings as these, it is not to be wondered at that many wrecks should strew the shores of literature. All that could be done under circumstances so discouraging has been done. If it be thought that we do not occupy the position we ought to occupy in these matters, the reason of it is apparent. It is to be hoped that it will not always be so. Literature has, in these days, become an honourable profession, the rewards of which are proportioned to the energy and skill of the workman, and are rarely conferred upon the undeserving. It is no longer a degraded means of earning bread. Genius is no longer left starving in the streets, or driven to the humiliating hunt for patronage. But that it is not so, is entirely owing to the fact that the people generally have made themselves its patrons. If, however, in this country, the people will persist in their cold indifference to their native literature, then we must expect to go back, and to see the days of Chatterton and Goldsmith return upon us. If men of letters cannot find the means of independence by the exercise of their pens, what must follow ? Either they must abandon their profession, or they must sink into a degraded life. In either case, a literature of our own becomes impossible.

" If the author be therefore still so necessary among us,"— said Goldsmith, in his *Inquiry into the state of Polite Learning*,— " let us treat him with proper consideration as a child of the public, not as a rent-charge on the community. And indeed a child of the public he is in all respects ; for while so well able to guide others, how incapable is he frequently found of guiding himself! His simplicity exposes him to all the insidious approaches of cunning ; his sensibility, to the slightest invasions of contempt.

Though possessed of fortitude to stand unmoved the expected bursts of an earthquake, yet of feelings so exquisitely poignant as to agonize under the slightest disappointment. Broken rest, tasteless meals, and causeless anxiety, shorten his life, or render it unfit for active employment ; prolonged vigils and intense application still further contract his span, and make his time glide insensibly away. Let us not then aggravate these natural inconveniences by neglect ; we have had sufficient instances of this kind already * * * *. It is enough that the age has already produced instances of men pressing foremost in the lists of fame, and worthy of better times, schooled by continued adversity into a hatred of their kind—flying from thought to drunkenness— yielding to the united pressure of labour, penury, and sorrow— sinking unheeded, without one friend to drop a tear on their unattended obsequies, and indebted to charity for a grave."

Goldsmith, however, did not suggest the proper remedy when he spoke of patronage by "the great." To depend on patronage is only a degree less galling than to depend on slavery. A man of self-respect would rather starve as a bookseller's hack than thrive as a rich man's shadow. The evil has been done away with by the natural course of events,—by the spread of civilization and the growth of intelligence among the great body of the people. No- where in Europe, where there exists a Literature, could the language just quoted be applied with any degree of truth in the present day. That it can be so applied to ourselves, must be regarded as a severe reproach. Men of genius have wandered through our streets without the means of earning bread, and have finally fled from our shores. Others have led a life which was nothing but a hopeless and protracted struggle. At whose doors must this misery be laid ? Not, certainly, at those of individuals ; but at those of the people who, possessing no generous or patriotic feeling, can regard such calamities with indifference. Where ten thousand a year, at least, can be devoted to the purchase of English periodicals, something ought to be spared for the maintenance of local ones. In asking that some means should be provided for the development of native talent, nothing is sought for that would be either humiliating to the receiver or burdensome to the giver. Literature requires neither charity nor patronage; it requires nothing but a generous appreciation from the public. That can be manifested only by the encouragement of literary publications. Such encouragement involves no tax upon modest means, and runs no risk of ingratitude; while it saves a country the disgrace of having starved and neglected the very men from whose names its greatest honour is derived.

But there are, obviously, other considerations besides those attaching to men of letters personally. Their fate may be passed over with indifference, as it has been already; but the matter does not end there. Injustice to the class means injury to the nation. If it is desirable that this country should not be known to the rest of the world simply in its commercial relations,—that it should, in due time, possess a literature of its own—how is this end to be accomplished? Unless a radical change takes place in the temper of the people, the prospects of an independent literature are extremely dim. If discouragement in its bitterest forms must always await the man of letters, the result must be injurious to our character as a community. No man will willingly enter upon a path which can only lead to suffering. We shall thus be left to rely helplessly upon the productions of another land, as we do at present; we shall produce nothing of our own beyond slavish imitations; we shall have to abandon all hope of originality in conception, of novelty in thought or style. This is not a prospect which any lover of his country can regard with pleasure. And let it be recollected that what is true of this Colony is equally true of our sister Colonies. Where, then, lies the hope of an Australian literature? It is time that Australia should begin to put forth some distinct evidence of mental power.

At present it is little more than a mart for the unsaleable produce of Paternoster Row. Patriotism has not yet developed itself amongst us; and the history of the world has shewn that where there has been no patriotism, there has never been a literature.

The condition of matters at the present time cannot be better described than in the words of Mr. Deniehy, quoted in Horne's *Australian Facts and Prospects*. Although written several years ago, the truth is by no means lessened by the lapse of time:— " In Sydney, the oldest of the Australian cities, and with those refinements and home feelings to which letters and art must always look for real recognition, purely literary pursuits are at a discount. The leading daily journal occasionally inserts a short article on subjects lying somewhat in the neighbourhood of æsthetics; but this is rather a matter of taste and liberality on the part of the proprietors than one of recognised demand on the part of readers. The graces and subtleties of literary art, except among a class of lettered *élite*, too small to be taken practically into calculation, are little cared for. The journalists likely to succeed in the particular work required are men of tolerably long residence in the country, practically acquainted with local characters and local things, and with the pens, in some instances perhaps of rough, but in all of ready writers. Of these we have quite as many as are likely to be needed for a long time." In fact, it cannot be said that literature has any recognized position here whatever. The number of those who profess it is small, and they are not animated by any spirit of brotherhood. There is no literary society. Several " Associations" have been formed from time to time, for the purpose of promoting an *esprit de corps*, but they never lasted.

In the matter of Libraries, we are thus situated. The oldest institution of the kind is the Australian Library, established in 1826, and now possessing 18,000 volumes. The collection consists principally of novels and other light reading, but it comprises some rare and valuable works, which are little appreciated. There is more of old English literature to be found in this library than in any other in the Colony. The number of subscribers is 300 ; too small a number to keep the institution out of difficulties. No attempt is consequently made to increase the books, otherwise than by a few recently published works, received by the monthly mail. The Mechanics' School of Arts, established in 1833, possesses a library of 13,000 volumes. This also consists mainly of novels and other branches of popular literature. The number of members is upwards of 1,000. The Parliamentary Library, established in 1843, contains nearly 16,000 volumes. It is one of the best in the Colony, but unfortunately, its use is confined strictly to Members of the Legislature. It contains a very good selection of books. The University Library numbers only 7,000 volumes. All of these are, of course, valuable works, but the collection of English literature is very deficient. It is with very great difficulty indeed that any old English work can be procured in the Colony. The booksellers import new books only. Their stock, as a rule, is not of a high class—consisting almost exclusively of such works as are likely to be attractive to miscellaneous readers. Few works that scholars would care to read can be found on their shelves. It is not true, as is sometimes said, that we are " not a reading people," but it is true that our reading is not of a very advanced description. The statistics given above, with respect to the circulation of English periodicals, illustrate this fact. A sum of money has been voted by the Legislature for the establishment of a Free Public Library, but no sign of such an institution is yet visible. It is sadly wanted ; for all our Libraries put together are not sufficient to meet the demands of a scholar. It may consequently be doubted whether there are six men in the Colony whose knowledge even of English Literature is anything more than a superficial one.

Few facts can speak more decisively as to the estimation in which learning is held among us, than the attendance at the classes of the University. There are three Professors—one of Classics, a second of Mathematics, and a third of Physics; and there are four Readers—one of Jurisprudence and Constitutional History, a second of the English Language and Literature, a third of the French Language and Literature, and a fourth of the German Language and Literature. The number of students matriculating in each year, from the commencement, is as follows :—

1852	24	1860	19
1853	14	1861	11
1854	10	1862	9
1855	11	1863	16
1856	1	1864	10
1857	19	1865	21
1858	7	1866	14
1859	5	Total	191

PERIODICAL LITERATURE.

I.—NEWSPAPERS.

1803.—The Sydney Gazette and New South Wales Advertiser. Published by Authority.

No. 1, Saturday, 5th March. Shortly after this date it was
published on Sundays. In the year 1825 it was published twice
a week; in the year 1827 it was published daily, subsequently
three times a week; and in the year 1842 it died. Its size was
enlarged at various times. At first it consisted of four pages of
small demy; then of two pages, with three columns in each, the
sheet being slightly larger; and lastly, of four pages of the
usual size.

The appearance of this publication, for some years after its
establishment, is the reverse of attractive. The paper is bad,
the types with which it was printed were evidently half worn out,
and the contents consist merely of advertisements, with a few
official announcements, and a sprinkling of local intelligence.
The printer, publisher, proprietor, and editor, was a man named
George Howe. This Caxton of our country was a creole, born
in St. Kitts, in the West Indies, where his father and brother
had for many years conducted the Government Press. He went
to London, and was engaged as a printer at several establishments; among others, at the office of the *Times*. He arrived
in this Colony in the year 1800; and, as there was no Press
established here at the time, he offered his services to the
Governor in the capacity of a printer. His proposal was
accepted; a small supply of materials was ordered from London,
and soon after its arrival, the publication of the *Gazette* com-

c

menced. It was conducted solely with a view to the service of the Government. What we may term the "leading article" in the first issue runs as follows :—

" The utility of a PAPER in the COLONY, as it must open a source of solid information, will, we hope, be universally felt and acknowledged. We have courted the assistance of the Ingenious and Intelligent :—we open no channel to political discussion, or Personal Animadversion : Information is our only Purpose : that accomplished, we shall consider that we have done our duty, in our exertions to merit the Approbation of the PUBLIC, and to secure a liberal Patronage to the SYDNEY GAZETTE."

The programme thus announced was faithfully adhered to. Up to the year 1823 the *Gazette* supplied its readers with nothing more lively than the Acts and Proceedings of the Government. In that year the Colonial Secretary, Major Goulburn, informed Mr. Howe that his columns might be opened to the public for political discussion ; and in the following year the censorship under which the paper had till then been carried on was abolished, and the "Liberty of the Press" was formally announced. This was due to the liberal policy adopted by the then Governor, Sir Thomas Brisbane.

The difficulties with which Howe had to contend in his printing operations were very great, and form an ample excuse for the poor appearance of his journal. The voyage to England in those days occupied many months ; the arrival of a ship was a rare event ; there was no commerce with other countries ; and consequently, when ink and paper fell short in the office of the *Gazette*, it was by no means easy to procure the necessary supplies. Many numbers were printed on paper of all sorts of colours ; green, blue, pink, and yellow, were almost as common as white ; but the prevailing tint is a dirty compromise between white and yellow. Inconveniencies of this kind seem to have existed for many years subsequently. The first specimen of good printing we meet with is the *Colonist*, a weekly newspaper published in 1835: the proprietor having brought out from England a large Columbian press, with a stock of excellent printing material.

The literary management of the *Gazette* never reflected much credit on the Colony. The small amount of original writing that appeared in its columns during its early years, proceeded from the pen of the proprietor. On his death, in 1821, the business was conducted by his son Robert, who was drowned, a few years after, while fishing in the harbour. The Rev. Ralph Mansfield then became the editor: he was also the proprietor and editor of the *New South Wales Magazine;* and he was, for many years, the editor of the *Herald.* His intellect was distinguished rather by its sound sense than by its brilliancy or polish. Mr. Mansfield was succeeded in the editorship of the *Gazette* by the Rev. H. Carmichael, a teacher of classics in the Australian College. He, however, gave offence to the proprietors by an article in which he commented on the large salaries paid to certain Government officials—the policy of the *Gazette* not admitting of any strictures on Government. His services were dispensed with, whereupon he brought an action for breach of agreement, and recovered £150 damages. The next editor was a man named O'Shaughnessy, who had been sent out to the Colony as a convict, and who was subsequently assigned to Howe. The latter employed him in the capacity of a reporter to his newspaper, and also as an occasional writer of leading articles. His appointment as responsible editor of the *Gazette* was strongly denounced by Dr. Lang, in the columns of his journal, the *Colonist.* The Doctor wrote a series of articles under the title of "The Literary Profession," in which he dwelt upon the dangerous results to morality likely to ensue from the writings of editorial convicts. The first of these articles was expressly aimed at O'Shaughnessy, and became the subject of an action at law. Dr. Lang defended his own case. His speech on the occasion is published at full length in the last edition of his *History of New South Wales*. O'Shaughnessy soon after ceased to act as editor of the *Gazette*; but whether on account of these exposures or not is uncertain. The *Gazette* itself ascribed his removal to his pecuniary embarrassments. The doubt is strengthened by the fact that the next editor of the paper was another and still more notorious convict—a man named Watt. The venerable champion of colonial morals was again in arms, the *Colonist* was again the medium of his assault, and Watt was eventually driven from the field. A full account of this individual may be found in Mudie's *Felonry*. Another editor of the *Gazette* was a Mr. Cavenagh. A curious squabble arose between him and Mr. W. C. Wentworth, the details of which are prominently noted in the papers of the time. A paragraph, slightly ridiculing the latter, appeared in the *Gazette*. Mr. Wentworth attributed it to the editor, and wrote a violent letter on the subject to the proprietors of the paper. Mr. Cavenagh brought an action for libel, and recovered £225 damages. No one was more given to the use of rough language than Mr. Wentworth, and it occasions some surprise to find that he felt it so acutely when applied to himself.

1824.—THE AUSTRALIAN. 4 pages.

No. 1, Thursday, 14th October. Published weekly; price, one shilling. Subsequently published twice a week.

Considerable interest attaches to this newspaper, from the connection which Mr. W. C. Wentworth maintained with it for many years. It may be said to have owed its existence to him, and he was long in the habit of contributing editorially to its columns. Mr. Wentworth was a native of the Colony, having been born in Norfolk Island, in the year 1791. He went to England, at the age of 26, for the purpose of education. He was a student at Cambridge; and while there, competed for the prize awarded to the best English Poem on " Australasia," in 1823.

The prize was gained by W. M. Praed, whose name is still remembered in English Literature; but Mr. Wentworth stood second on a list of twenty-five. Previously to this achievement, he published, in 1819, a history of his native country, of which an account will be found in another part of this narrative. He was called to the Bar in London, and returned to the Colony in the year 1824, when he commenced practice both as a barrister and an attorney, there being no division of the profession at that time.

The origin of the *Australian* is thus described in a memoir of Mr. Wentworth, published twenty-three years ago :—" Being shortly after this (1819) called to the Bar, Mr. Wentworth became acquainted with the late Dr. Wardell, who was the editor and proprietor of a London evening newspaper called the *Statesman*. This gentleman accompanied Mr. Wentworth to Sydney, in the year 1824, bringing with them materials for the purpose of starting a newspaper in Sydney. This was the origin of the *Australian*, a publication which rendered the State some service ; and after many hazardous changes, still (1843) continues to flourish. Mr. Wentworth, however, soon relinquished his share of the publication, and devoted himself with success to the more lucrative practice of his profession." In his Account of the Colony, Mr. Wentworth published a number of the *Sydney Gazette*, and expressed the following opinion with regard to it, and also to the necessity for another journal in the Colony. " Here also is a weekly newspaper called the *Sydney Gazette and New South Wales Advertiser*. The *matériel* of this paper belongs, I believe, exclusively to Government ; hence arises that right of censorship which the Colonial Secretary has hitherto exercised over it ; hence, too, the cause why it seldom contains any interesting matter, except the public Acts of the local Government, for the notification of which it serves as the vehicle. Anything in the shape of political discussion is a novelty which it is rarely permitted to exhibit. An independent paper, therefore, which may serve to point out the rising interests of the colonists, and become the organ of their grievances and rights, their wishes and wants, is highly necessary ; and, it is to be hoped, will speedily be set on foot."

It would appear, from these extracts, that Mr. Wentworth had formed the design, while in London, of starting a newspaper on his return to the Colony. While thus connected with the *Australian*, Mr. Wentworth was engaged in rendering those services to his fellow countrymen which have made his name a household word among them to the present day. The political and social state of the Colony was essentially different in those days from what it is now. It was so different, indeed, that it is hard for us to realise it. Socially, the inhabitants of the Colony were divided into two parties, the "Emancipists" and the "Exclusives," who were as bitterly opposed to each other as the *Neri* and *Bianchi* of Florence in the thirteenth century. Politically, Government was administered on principles approaching to those of a pure despotism, mildly tempered with the epigrams of the *Australian* and the *Monitor*. There was no representation of the people in Parliament—there was no trial by Jury in the Law Courts—there was no freedom of the Press in the printing offices. To obtain these advantages for the country, Mr. Wentworth laboured unceasingly. He was at the head of every movement made for that purpose. His eloquence was unsparingly exerted in the cause of political and social independence. In his hands, the *Australian* was an engine of no slight importance for the accomplishment of his views ; and rarely has the importance of an unfettered Press been more signally exhibited than in the case of that journal. How his connection with it came to an end has been related by himself, in words which afford a striking illustration of the social state of the Colony at the time. In a speech delivered by him in the Legislative Council, in August,

1843, when opposing the election, as Speaker, of the late Mr. Alexander Macleay, a man of some distinction, he said:—
"The second act of this Goverument, of which the Honorable Member was Prime Minister and the most active agent, was to introduce a penal clause into an Act, that any person guilty of blasphemy, or of a seditious libel, should be subject to banishment from the Colony. It seemed to him that the laws of England were sufficiently stringent to meet cases of that kind, and that there was no necessity for local enactments. But there were particular individuals in the eye of the Government to whom the banishment clause was intended to apply, and they were himself and his lamented colleague, Dr. Wardell. Just at that time, his professional occupation pressed upon him so much that he had very little leisure either for sedition or blasphemy, but the clause in the Act was so exceedingly wide, that he clearly saw, if he continued with the Press, he should not be long before he should subject himself to the heaviest penalties; in fact, the clause would catch any one who dared to write a word against the Government, and he thought best to retire. He, therefore, made a present of his share in the concern to his colleague, Dr. Wardell, who carried it on for a year or two longer, and soon found himself, as he expected, involved in prosecutions at the instance of the Government. He sold the paper, and, in a short time, the purchaser was lodged in the same gaol where Mr. Hall, the conductor of the only other liberal journal in the Colony, was incarcerated."

Dr. Wardell, here alluded to, was a barrister holding a degree of Doctor of Laws, and a man of high capacity. He acted as chief Editor of the *Australian*, and adopted the same line of politics as Mr. Wentworth. In an old periodical, called the *South Asian Register*, published in 1828, occurs the following:—
"The *Australian* has sold 600 copies twice a week, it is said, and the copyright was recently disposed of for £3,600, to eight

shareholders, by Dr. Wardell." Dr. Wardell then retired from political and public life, and a few years after was shot by bushrangers. Some interesting particulars concerning him may be found in Therry's *Reminiscences*. A gentleman named Hayes succeeded Dr. Wardell as the editor of the *Australian*. In 1829 he was convicted of a seditious libel upon the Government, for having asserted, in his journal, that the Governor had, in a certain case which excited much sensation, substituted his own arbitrary will for the law. He was sentenced to six months' imprisonment, a fine of £100, and compelled to find securities for his good behaviour for three years. The *Australian* subsequently passed into the hands of Mr. G. R. Nichols, an attorney, who possessed the reputation of a wit. He was a native of the Colony, was distinguished for his ability and his patriotism, and on the introduction of Responsible Government in 1856, formed one of the first Ministry under it, holding office as Auditor General. His death took place in the following year. The last number of the *Australian* was published on the 28th September, 1848.

1825.—Howe's Weekly Commercial Express.

No. 1, Monday, 25th May. This journal expired with its twenty-second number. The proprietor, Robert Howe, was also the proprietor of the *Gazette*, which had recently begun to make its appearance twice a week. He found it impossible to carry on both publications at the same time, and accordingly was compelled to sacrifice the *Express*.

1826.—The Monitor. 8 pages.

No. 1, Friday, 19th May. Published weekly; subsequently twice a week; price, one shilling.

This journal was started by a gentleman named Edward Smith Hall, who was not only proprietor, but editor, printer, and publisher as well. It played a very important part in the political and social struggles of the time. During the Governorship of General Darling, which lasted to 1831, the *Monitor* was engaged in violent opposition to the acts of his Government. In this opposition it was supported by its cotemporary the *Australian*, under the vigorous editorship of Dr. Wardell. Governor Darling appears to have been extremely sensitive to newspaper criticism. He made every effort in his power to get rid of his torturers, but he never succeeded in doing so. At one time he endeavoured to pass an Act—commonly called "the gagging Act"—by which every newspaper published in the Colony would be required to obtain a license from the Government, to be renewed every year; and also to pay a stamp duty of fourpence for every issue. In this object he was defeated by the Chief Justice, Mr. Forbes, whose sanction it was necessary to obtain before any Act of the Legislature could come into force. Mr. Forbes regarded the proposed measure as unconstitutional, and declined to give it his official approbation. The Governor then instituted criminal proceedings against the editors of the opposition Press. Libel actions became so frequent during the years 1828 and 1829, that the Supreme Court, it is said, was almost wholly occupied in hearing them. Mr. Hall appeared seven times in the dock. He was sentenced to pay heavy fines, amounting to several hundreds of pounds, and to endure terms of imprisonment amounting to three years and a half. These measures, however, were not effectual. The papers continued to pour forth their torrents of invective, and, if more cautious, were hardly less virulent than before.

These journals certainly exhibited very little regard to the decencies of discussion. Their language was frequently so violent as to be quite unjustifiable. The bitterness of their opposition was commented on in the House of Commons, by gentlemen not at all disposed to support the cause of the Governor. Dr. Lang, an experienced journalist himself, gives the following character of them in his History of the Colony :—

" It was unfortunate, however, for the colonial public, that the opposition papers of the Colony, during the government of General Darling, were by no means distinguished for that scrupulous regard to truth without which no person can merit the confidence of the public. There was a rabid desire to publish whatever had a tendency to bring either the Governor, or persons in any way connected with the Government, into general disfavour ; and information of this kind was accordingly received with the utmost eagerness, and often without the least regard to the character of the quarter from which it came."

It is but right to add, that the official journal provoked much of this misconduct on the part of its cotemporaries. It was servile towards the Government, and scurrilous towards all who opposed it.

1827.—THE GLEANER. 4 pages.

No. 1, 9th April. Published weekly.

This was a very unpretending publication, started by Dr. Halloran, whose son, Henry Hallorau, has for many years past distinguished himself by his poetical writings. Dr. Halloran appears to have been a poet also, as there is mention of a volume of poems published by him in 1806. The *Gleaner* was not calculated to compete successfully with its vigorous cotemporaries, and its existence seems to have been very short.

1831.—* THE SYDNEY HERALD.

No. 1, Monday, 18th April. This journal was at first published weekly as a small sheet of four pages ; in 1836 it was published twice a week ; in 1837 three times a week ; and in 1841, daily. It remained for twelve years the only daily paper in the country. In 1842 it was enlarged in size, and called *The Sydney*

---

* The journals to which an asterisk is prefixed are still in existence.

Morning Herald, by which name it is now known to the world. In 1853 it was again enlarged, appearing as a double sheet of eight pages instead of four.

A leading article in this journal, published on the 2nd January, 1843, gives some interesting information as to its position at that now distant period, and also as to the position of other publications. After alluding to the commercial depression which has given a gloomy celebrity in our annals to the year 1842, it proceeds to say,—" The adversity of the past year was, of course, felt by the Press, as well as by other interests. To four of our cotemporaries, indeed, it proved fatal. The *Free Press* and *Examiner*, after a very brief but noisy career, gave up the ghost; the *Monitor*, having lost the master-hand which had from the first guided its affairs, had reached the respectable age of sixteen years, when it too slept the sleep of death ; and even the poor old *Sydney Gazette*, the first literary adventurer in the southern hemisphere, after a long and eventful life of nearly forty years, sank into an inglorious grave. Once the defunct veteran was exhumed, and an effort made to re-animate the vital spark, but in vain—the decree had gone forth, and could not be revoked." With respect to itself, the editor states that " the circulation of the *Herald* still exceeded 3,000 numbers daily, or 940,000 in the year; the number of separate advertisements published during the previous year was about 18,000, representing a total of insertions amounting to the prodigious number of 54,000."

The lapse of twenty-three years has added largely to its prosperity and influence. Its daily circulation is now rated at 8,450. As for its advertisements, they are so numerous that it would not be easy to calculate the total number of insertions in the year. On Saturdays, the ordinary eight pages of the journal are almost entirely occupied with advertisements, thus rendering it necessary to publish an additional sheet of four pages. In addition to the daily issue, a weekly edition is published every Saturday, for circulation through the country; it consists of twelve pages, and the number of subscribers is about 11,500. On the departure of the mail steamers for Europe, a " Summary" of the *Herald* is published, consisting of no less than sixteen pages. Some 14,000 copies are usually sold on these occasions. There is no other journal in Australia that favours the public with such a mass of print as this.

During the early period of its existence, the *Herald* was principally edited by the Rev. Ralph Mansfield, of whom mention has already been made. For the last ten years or so, his place has been occupied by the Rev. John West, author of a " History of Tasmania," in 2 vols. 8vo., published in 1852. Mr. West is a powerful writer, on certain topics. Some of his compositions, especially where sarcasm comes into play, are admirable specimens of style. But, as a rule, the leading articles of the *Herald* are not distinguished by their brilliancy. Curiously enough, although this journal has been, and is, far more successful than any other in the Colony, it has never possessed any reputation for literary ability. Its success is entirely owing to the policy adopted by its proprietors; to the fullness of its commercial, and the accuracy of its local, intelligence. On this point, the following passage, taken from the *Colonist* of 1837, deserves attention:—

"If we are not misinformed, the freedom with which the *Herald* launched out, in 1834 or 5, in its attacks upon Colonial Whiggism, was immediately followed by the most marked demonstrations: hundreds of subscribers withdrew their patronage; hundreds of new subscribers as promptly flowed in; and the balance between the two showed a net gain to the extent of several hundreds. If this was really the case—and we have sufficient reason for believing it was—it amounted to a sort of 'polling' of public opinion on the question at issue. The *Herald*, from its commencement, has enjoyed a wider circulation than any of its cotemporaries, and may be said to have fairly *pervaded* the population. And the result of its unflinching advocacy of Colonial Toryism has been—not general abandonment—but an extent of patronage, both in circulation and advertisements, with which no other Sydney journal can compare."

The line of politics thus early advocated by the *Herald* has been steadily pursued up to the present time. Its Toryism has increased in a direct ratio to the Radicalism of the Constitution, and its prosperity has increased in a direct ratio to its Toryism. The fact is striking and important. It might have been imagined that, however profitable the advocacy of Toryism may have been in former times, it would have ceased to be so on the introduction of universal suffrage and the triumph of " Liberalism." Since that period, Toryism, as a political element in the State, has almost become extinct. No trace of its influence can be observed in the character of our legislation. But the fact is precisely the reverse. Universal suffrage seems to have operated largely in its favour. The more determined the opposition of the *Herald* to the prevailing politics of the day, the more has it grown in favour with those whose support is most valuable to a journal. Without the slightest power to influence an election or to affect the tone of a debate, it continues to enlarge its subscription list and swell the number of its advertisements. The explanation, no doubt, is easy enough. The masses, in whose hands all political power is lodged, rarely subscribe and never advertise. But the merchants and the shopkeepers, who never go to the hustings, are all readers and all advertisers. The consequence is, that while the daily journal which almost dictates the political government of the country is very poorly supported in comparison with its rival, the latter, without any political influence at all, is daily increasing in wealth and circulation.

1831.—THE SYDNEY TIMES. 4 pages.

No. 1, 1st January. Published twice a week. This paper was edited by the proprietor, N. L. Kentish, and lived for several years, although it does not seem to have been either a very powerful organ or a very successful speculation. In 1836, the proprietor made affidavit that the circulation amounted to nearly 1,000 copies of each issue. In 1837, it congratulated the public " upon the addition made to Colonial literature, by the *Literary News* and *Temperance Magazine*, and by the extension of the *Colonist* to a twice-a-week paper, under the auspices of its talented founder, and also upon the revival of the *Australian Monthly Magazine*."

1832.—HILL'S LIFE IN NEW SOUTH WALES. 4 pages.

No. 1, Friday, 6th July. Published weekly. This journal was published by a person named Hill, who had been a printer in the *Monitor* office. It possessed no peculiar features, and it perished in the following year.

1832.—*NEW SOUTH WALES GOVERNMENT GAZETTE. Published by Authority.

No. 1, 7th March. This is a purely official publication, and it still exists in that character.

1832.—THE CURRENCY LAD. 4 pages.

No. 1, Saturday, August 25. Published weekly. This periodical, as its name implies, professed to be the organ of the native-born population. It makes a very poor appearance. It was " edited, printed, and published, by Horatio Wills, an Australian, joint proprietor with the executors and executrix of the late R. Howe, at the *Gazette* office." The *Currency Lad* has left no name behind it ; it was merely one of many periodicals commenced without any rational expectation of success.

1835.—THE ALFRED.

A newspaper of this name is mentioned in the Almanac for the year 1835, as existing in Sydney, but no copy of it can be found.

1835.—THE COLONIST ; *a weekly Journal of Politics, Commerce, Agriculture, Literature, Science, and Religion, for the Colony of New South Wales.* 8 pages.

No. 1, Thursday, 1st January, subsequently (1837) published twice a week. This publication was set on foot by the Rev Dr. Lang, a gentleman who has occupied a very prominent position in public life for the last forty years. He was born in Scotland, in the year 1799, and arrived in this Colony iu 1823. Siuce that period, he has been indefatigably engaged, not ouly in the performance of his dnties as a minister of religion, but in the bitter struggles of political life, in unceasing labonrs with his pen, and in various efforts to improve the social condition of the Colony. He has been an active Member of the Legislature, both under the old form of Government and the new. He was the first, or one of the first, to introduce into the Colony a higher class of emigrants from the old world than that which had previously reached our shores. He was the means of establishing the first educational institution of any importance in the Colony. As a writer, he is by far the most voluminous we have to boast of. An account of his various productions will be found in other portions of this narrative. For the present, we are concerned only with his journalistic career. This commenced with the *Colonist*. So far as appearance is concerned, no previously established journal can compare with it— the paper and the printing beiug both excellent. In the selection of its contents, also, it shewed a greater appreciation of the claims of literature, apart from politics, than any of its cotemporaries. The first number contained the following account of its origin :— " Towards the close of the year 1831, the Rev. Dr. Lang returned to this Colony from England, with an order from the Right Honorable the Secretary of State for the Colonies, for a grant of money from the Colonial Treasury for the establishment of a College in Sydney, together with several scientific and literary men to act as head masters or professors, and a large number of Scotch mechanics, of a reputable character and superior ability, to erect the requisite buildings." This refers to the well-known " Australian College." It is further stated that the scheme thus propounded was violently opposed by the different journals then established in Sydney, viz., the *Sydney Gazette*, the *Australian*, the *Monitor*, and the *Sydney Herald*, and that the *Colonist* was called into existence for the purpose of repelling their attacks. Alluding to this matter in his History, the Doctor says : " It was the incessant assault and battery to which I was subjected for years together by these unprincipled journals, and the serious pecuniary loss in which it involved me, from the withdrawal of public support from our Institution, that induced me on a subsequent occasion to avail myself of the aid of the Press, and to establish a weekly journal on other and better principles, and with higher and nobler views. And, I am happy to add, I have uniformly found that, so long as I have had that powerful engine at my command, it has always been comparatively easy to keep the whole pack of colonial dogs at bay." The columns of the *Colonist* were employed by Dr. Lang, not alone in waging his own battles with the numberless enemies that were always hovering round his camp and cutting off his baggage, but in asserting the claims of morality and religion. It died in 1840.

1835.—COMMERCIAL JOURNAL AND ADVERTISER. 4 pages.

Published twice a week.

In January, 1839, this publication, which, as its name implies, paid more attention to commercial matters than to anything else, was enlarged in size, and appeared as a new series. At the commencement of 1841, having passed into new hands, it came out as the *Free Press and Commercial Journal*, edited by Mr. M'Eachern, who had acted as editor of the *Colonist* at the time of its decease.

1837.—Bent's News and New South Wales Advertiser.

This publication ceased in July, 1839, with its 172nd issue. In his "Farewell Address," the proprietor states that he had sold his copyright to a joint stock company, established for the purpose of bringing out a new journal under the title of *The Australasian Chronicle.*

1839.—The Standard.

No. 1.—7th January.

This appears to have been a sectarian paper, established in the interest of what is called the "High Church" Party of the Church of England.

1839.—The Australasian Chronicle.   4 pages.

No. 1, Friday, 2nd August, published weekly; and subsequently twice and three times a week.

This publication was also devoted to sectarian purposes. They are thus alluded to in an editorial statement in the first issue :—" To explain and uphold the civil and religious principles of the Catholics, and to maintain their rights, will be the primary objects of the *Australasian Chronicle*." It was edited for some years by Mr. Duncan, an able and industrious journalist of the time, who now holds the office of Collector of Customs at Sydney.   The *Chronicle* presents a very favourable appearance among its cotemporaries, especially for a sectarian journal. Its title was subsequently altered, and it then appeared as the *Morning Chronicle.*   This designation was also changed; and, in July, 1846, it appeared as the *Sydney Chronicle.*   Its term of existence was rather a lengthened one.

D

1840.—The Temperance Advocate, and Australasian Commercial and Agricultural Intelligencer. 4 pages.

No. 1, October 7.

A weekly sheet, devoted to the cause of temperance, and " printed and published for John Fairfax, the editor and proprietor, of Spring-street, by James Reading, at the office of the *Temperance Advocate*, King-street, Sydney."

1841.—The Omnibus and Sydney Spectator. 8 pages.

No. 1, Saturday, 2nd October. Published weekly.

This publication endeavoured to obtain popularity by humorous comments on the events of the day, but it does not appear to have succeeded to any marked extent.

1841.—The Colonial Observer: *a weekly Journal of Politics, Commerce, Agriculture, Literature, Science, and Religion, for the Colony of New South Wales.* 8 pages.

No. 1, Thursday, 7th October.

This was another sectarian journal, devoted to the advocacy of " Evangelical Protestantism," and to rather violent attacks on the " Papal System." The war among the religious sects of the day seems to have been carried on with excessive bitterness. The *Observer* was edited by the Rev. Dr. Lang.

1842.—The Teetotaller, and General Newspaper. 4 pages.

No. 1, Saturday, 8 January.

A similar publication to the foregoing. The 89th number (27th September, 1843) states:—" With this number we close our labours, at least for the present. Like its predecessor and harbinger, the *Temperance Advocate*, the *Teetotaller* has been, in a pecuniary point of view, a losing concern, and that from the beginning."

1842.—THE NEW SOUTH WALES EXAMINER.   4 pages.

Published thrice a week.

1843.—THE SUN, AND NEW SOUTH WALES INDEPENDENT PRESS.
4 pages.

No. 1, Saturday, 28 January.   Published weekly.   Price, 3d.

This paper was apparently intended for circulation among the working classes.   It appears to have been in existence as a daily paper previous to the above date, the proprietor stating that, " owing to unforeseen difficulties in the mechanical department of his establishment, he has been reluctantly constrained to forego the continuance of his journal as a daily publication." The *Sun* was very free in its comments on passing affairs.

1843.—DUNCAN'S WEEKLY REGISTER OF POLITICS, FACTS, AND
GENERAL LITERATURE.   12 pages, 4to.

No. 1, Saturday, July 29.   This journal expired on the 27th December, 1845, with its 127th number.   The period during which it strove to exist was one of unexampled depression in commercial and monetary matters.   Every interest, every form of enterprise, in the Colony, was either partially or wholly paralyzed, and newspapers shared the general fate.   Politically, the *Register* was opposed to the squatters, who at that time formed a powerful class in the State, headed as they were by the most talented men of the day, and supported by the leading journals.   It was not powerful enough to cope with their celebrated organ, the *Atlas ;* but the support rendered by it to the Government was so far appreciated that, on its termination, Mr. Duncan was appointed Collector of Customs at Moreton Bay, and subsequently removed to Sydney.   During its existence, the editor endeavoured, as far as possible, to impart a literary interest to his publication ; the poets of the Colony—Messrs. Harpur, Halloran, Parkes, and others, were frequent contributors to its pages ; while reviews and notices of books were introduced at every opportunity.

1843.—The Sydney Record.   8 pages.

No. 1. Saturday, 7 October.   Published weekly.

The literary department of this paper was announced to be under the management of Mr. Arden, who had recently started a magazine in Sydney.   The *Record* was a weekly journal of general character.

1843.—The Satirist.

The editor of this paper was a Dr. Revel Johnson, a man of some notoriety in his day as a humourist.   He was criminally prosecuted for libel, and sentenced to two years' imprisonment.

Flanagan's History of the Colony has the following passage on the matter :—

"In the course of this year, the editor of an obscene publication called the *Satirist*, which had been circulated for some time in the city, was prosecuted in the name of the Crown, by the Attorney General; and having been found guilty under the statute intended for the suppression of publications dangerous to the public morals, was sentenced to two years' imprisonment. The printer and the publisher were severally punished with twelve months' loss of liberty. The publication was universally admitted to be a disgrace to the city, and how it came to receive patronage sufficient to prolong its career, even for the brief period during which it was permitted to exist, could hardly be accounted for, except on the ground that a reprehensible curiosity led to its being purchased by people who abhorred its contents. The editor (Dr. Revel Johnson) was a surgeon, who, being too much a man of fashion for his legitimate calling, sought to obtain at once a livelihood and a degree of celebrity, by bringing to the surface that vileness which ought to be permitted to remain shrouded in its appropriate veil of obscurity."

1843.—The Shipping Gazette, and Sydney General Trade List.

A purely commercial publication, issued by the proprietors of the *Herald*.   It appeared every Monday, and lasted for thirteen years; ceasing at the end of 1860.   Its contents were then transferred to the *Sydney Mail*, a weekly edition of the *Herald*.

1844.—THE ATLAS.   12 pages.

No. 1, Saturday, November 30.   Published weekly.

Among the many journals established in this Colony from the days of the *Gazette* to the present time, there is not one that can be said to have surpassed the *Atlas* in point of literary ability. Its contributors were among the ablest and most celebrated men of the day ; and at the head of them was Mr. Robert Lowe, recently a member of Lord Palmerston's Cabinet.   Mr. Lowe arrived in this Colony in the year 1842, and during his residence in Sydney he practised at the bar.   He was also a Member of the Legislative Council.   Another of its contributors was Mr. James Martin, then an attorney.   He was born in Ireland, in 1820, came to this Colony when a child, received his education here, and has now risen to the highest distinction as a lawyer and a politician.   He was called to the bar in 1856, on his appointment as Attorney General under the first Cowper Ministry ; was appointed a Queen's Counsel shortly after ; became Prime Minister of the Colony in 1863, and again in 1866.   A third contributor was Mr. William Forster, who at that time was a squatter.   He was born in Madras, in 1818, and arrived in this Colony eleven years afterwards.   For some years past he has been a distinguished Member of the Assembly.   In 1859 he was Colonial Secretary and Prime Minister, and in 1863 Colonial Secretary again.

The early numbers of the *Atlas* contain several poetical pieces by Mr. Lowe.   They consist principally of a series of " Descriptive Sketches," the descriptions referring to the scenery of Switzerland.   As Mr. Lowe has since become one of the most distinguished men in England, the following specimen of his earlier productions will be read with interest, if not with admiration :—

THE MOON.

When infant earth,
In might and mirth,
Burst from the chain that bound her;
I sprang from her breast,
Like a bird from the nest,
To hover for ever around her.

I shed my power
O'er many an hour,
When labour and grief are still;
And the tides of ocean,
In wildest commotion,
Are swayed like a child at my will.

Full many a child
Of genius wild,
Has basked in my noon of glory;
And drunk a thought
Which noon has wrought,
To a theme of deathless story.

And many a maiden
With love o'erladen,
Has sat with her lute beside her;
And caught a bliss
From my pearly kiss,
Which warmer lips denied her.

Yet rather gaze
On the blinding rays
Of the sun in noon-tide splendour,
Than bathe in the streams
Of my wizard dreams,
Though soft be their glance and tender!

For a withering pain
Shall shrivel thy brain,
In the midst of thy hour of gladness;
And the bow that wafts
My piercing shafts,
Is strung by the hand of madness!

I saw the pall
Of vapours fall,
On that doomed and silent earth;
When Ocean broke
His iron yoke,
I heard the earthquake's mirth.

I could not trace
On Earth's pale face,
The shadows of land and deep ;
For the shoreless wave
Of Nature's grave,
I saw, and I could not weep.

For fear and sorrow
New wings must borrow,
Ere they soar to my old, calm shrine ;
Man's pigmy race
Has dale and place,
But, other, far other is mine.

Yon Sun may shine
To ripen the vine,
And call up the seed that is sown ;
Let him serve like a slave,
The child of the grave,
I shine for myself alone.

Full many a change,
Drear, wild, and strange,
I've seen in my parent's form ;
When the curdling mould
Of a world grown old,
Was stirred by the breath of the storm.

Yet still did I speed
On my way without heed,
Nor mourned for the wreck that was doing ;
For my calm, cold light,
Is my own delight,
And I smile o'er the ashes of ruin.

Mr. Lowe also wrote a series of political sketches, under the
title of " Australian Frescoes." To make an imaginary painting
the means of ridiculing the chief subjects of political satire at
the time, was an ingenious idea, and the idea was gracefully
executed. It has been still better executed, however, by Mr.
Deniehy, in the *Southern Cross* of 1860. Indeed, Mr. Lowe does
not seem to have shone much in any kind of writing that required
invention. His principal contributions to the *Atlas* were leading

articles on political topics, and these are said to have been quite as good as any of his subsequent contributions to the London *Times*.

Mr. Martin's contributions to the *Atlas* were all anonymous. It may be taken for granted that they possessed no ordinary merit. Mr. Fowler wrote, in the *Month*, that "when the *Atlas* was established, Mr. Martin largely contributed to its columns, and by the dash and point of his articles proved himself a journalist of no mean powers. He was ultimately appointed editor of the paper, which he conducted most ably for two years." The same writer also states that Mr. Martin published a book of essays; that he subsequently started a magazine; and that in 1851, he wrote for a short time in the *Empire*.

With respect to Mr. Forster's writings, the following account of them appeared in the *Southern Cross* of 1860 :—

"In these days it was that, during the contest of the Crown tenants with Sir George Gipps, he commenced a literary career fertile of results for the local Press. Many of the most remarkable contributions to the *Atlas*, the organ of the pastoral party, were Mr. Forster's. His literary vigour in those days loved to display itself in the squib; and we suspect that the merit of many of his pungent trifles was pretty generally given, by readers of the *Atlas*, to the Right Honourable Robert Lowe, then understood to be at the head of the journal. Those who read *The Devil and the Governor* (a dramatic scene, in which Sir George Gipps was made to take his diabolical highness into council), little imagined that the writer was a sallow, thin, saturnine looking young gentleman, if more remarkable for one external characteristic than another, for a remarkably unassuming manner, who amused himself in "spells" from hard backwood toil in the wild, lonesome depths of a forest, *cutting* as it were, rather than writing, his sarcastic couplets, on the granitic obduracy of the Gipps' administrative policy. As a writer of squibs, we think Mr. Forster, on the whole, the most successful of practitioners in that vocation which makes gibing and jeering a fine art. Other literary men in New South Wales there are, who throw off this kind of politico-literary pyrotechny in forms of higher finish, with a grace and a fancy that would have pleased Winthrop Praed, or even the great master of metrical squibbery, Tom

Moore himself; but as a squib should be as generally understood as a proverb or a party-cry, we think these learned gentlemen of the Court of Momus commit an error in art—the sarcasm is too subtle and refined for any but well educated readers.—But, as a literary man, Mr. Forster has distinguished himself in higher and graver capacities than as a writer of sparkling *jeux d'esprit*. In journalism, he has flung into circulation some of the soundest political thinking on leading Australian topics that our country possesses. His contributions to the elder *Empire* evinced, uniformly, a remarkable faculty of dealing with the principles at the root of problems in politics; and also, a masterly power, not only in showing the errors of opponents, but in tracking the train of reasoning by which they had come to the wrong conclusion. His polemics in ecclesiastical polity, in the *Church Sentinel*, scarcely come within the scope of our criticism, but they deserve allusion, as showing the thorough liberalism of the present Prime Minister. As a poet, Mr. Forster's efforts have not been very ambitious, principally occasional rhymes, but always originating in, or instinct with, some great purpose. Irrespective of the character of the productions themselves, it may be, talking of the poetic faculty in the abstract, that Mr. Forster ranks with none of the loftier order, but the faculty is truly poetic, nevertheless; as John Sterling said, if we recollect rightly, of Charles Lamb, ' The gold in a spangle may be as sterling as that of a doubloon.' And again, as to the question of dimensions, it may be that the thing is small, not because the artificer has no more of the precious metal in his possession, but that he has neither mood nor market for working a larger quantity up."

These remarks, written by a very friendly pen, are followed by a series of sonnets by Mr. Forster. A sonnet hardly affords a sufficient test, to enable one to gauge the merit of a poet. Mr. Forster's neither rise above, nor sink below, the ordinary level of that class of compositions.

The *Atlas* carried on a very bitter and uncompromising war with the Governor of the day, Sir George Gipps. His policy was unfavourable to the interests of the squatters, and on their behalf the *Atlas* omitted no opportunity of opposing him. This opposition was conducted with better taste than that of the *Monitor* towards Governor Darling; but it is difficult, in the present day, to realise a state of society in which the supreme Head of the State is subjected to unceasing ridicule and abuse. The *Atlas* was, in some respects, an imitation of the London newspaper of that name; but this imitation did not affect the originality or the spirit of its contents. These were extremely varied and entertaining. Considerable space was devoted to the literature of the day, in the shape of reviews and extracts; political "squibs" in verse and prose, appeared in every number; and a couple of columns were devoted to a "Punch," one half being a "Sydney ingredient," consisting of original witticisms, and the other a "London ingredient," consisting of extracts from the London *Punch*. The printing and the paper are both unobjectionable; and altogether, this journal may be compared with any weekly newspaper that has ever been published. Notwithstanding its merit, it failed to secure a permanent existence. It expired at the end of 1848, having lived only four years and a half.

1844.—THE GUARDIAN: *a Weekly Journal of Politics, Commerce, Agriculture, Literature, Science, and Art, for the Middle and Working Classes of New South Wales.*

No. 1, Saturday, 16 March. 8 pages.

This paper declared itself to be the organ of a Society called "The Mutual Protection Association," and explained its political creed under the title of "Constitutional Radicalism." The following passage from its first leading article will give an idea of its character:—

"The question for the middle and working classes of New South Wales to consider is this—Are the dominant influence and oligarchical sway of an upstart and selfish aristocracy of mere wealth likely to prove conducive to the interests, the liberty, and prosperity of the people?"

And again :—

"It is to the working classes especially that we look for the direct and substantial support which will be immediately available for the recurring exigencies of our undertaking. The *Guardian* is not only their own accredited organ and special advocate, but it is their property, an engine of their creation, and dependent on themselves alone for its existence, its independence, and its incorruptibility. The system of credit has been the bane of newspaper undertakings in this Colony, and rendered it a matter of enormous outlay to establish a paper. These difficulties we propose to surmount by the simple expedient, now almost universal in England, of the news-vending system."

1845.—* BELL'S LIFE IN SYDNEY. 4 pages.

No. 1, Saturday, 4th January. Published weekly.

A sporting journal. The principal contributor for many years was Mr. G. R. Morton, a nephew of a well-known London farce writer. He possesses considerable talent for humour, and is now editor of *Sydney Punch*.

1845.—THE SOUTHERN REPORTER.

No. 1, Saturday, 4 January.

On the appearance of this publication, its cotemporary the *Sentinel* spoke of it as "a sort of journal called the *Southern Reporter*, the object of which seems to be the support of the monstrosities of Popery, and the promotion of the favourite crotchet of O'Connell—Repeal."

1845.—THE SENTINEL. 4 pages.

No. 1, Wednesday, 8 January. Published weekly.

A sectarian organ, apparently in the interest of the Church of England. Its remarks on cotemporary "Papists" and "Puseyites" were rather strong. It seems to have been a continuation of Dr. Lang's *Colonial Observer*.

1845.—THE SOUTHERN QUEEN.

No. 1, January. Published weekly.

The only information I can obtain respecting this periodical is from a critical notice of it published in the *Atlas* of the 4th January, and from another in the *Sentinel* of the 8th. It was pronounced by the former journal to be worthless. The *Sentinel* speaks of it as a journal "distinguished by eminent ability and general good taste.. The 'Introductory Address' is one of the most spirited and talented articles that ever issued from the Australian Press." In subsequent issues, the *Sentinel* abused it on the score of its religious opinions.

1845.—THE EXAMINER, *Political, Literary, and Commercial Journal.* 8 pages.

From a prospectus published in this paper, it appears to have been a new series of another paper called the *Commercial Journal and General Advertiser.* It is stated to have been edited by Mr. Richard Thomson, "late editor of the *Atlas.*"

1845.—COMMERCIAL JOURNAL AND GENERAL ADVERTISER. 4 pages.

No. 1, Saturday, 5th April.

Very well printed and edited, but not successful.

1845.—THE AGE. 4 pages. Price, 1½d.

No. 1, April.

A creditable attempt to establish a cheap periodical, but it met with no success.

1846.—THE SPECTATOR. 12 pages.

No. 1, Saturday, 24th January. Published weekly.

A well-written weekly paper, apparently started on behalf of the squatters. Its term of existence was limited to a year or so.

1846.—THE TEMPERANCE HERALD.

1847.—WEEKLY DISPATCH. 8 pages.

No. 1, Saturday, 3rd July.

Another attempt to establish a weekly journal, but as unsuccessful as the rest.

1847.—THE HEADS OF THE PEOPLE.

An illustrated miscellany of a humourous character, published weekly. It contained portraits of public men; the drawings being lithographed by the proprietor, Baker, a lithographer by trade. This publication was not a brilliant production, but it was amusing and tolerably successful. It lasted nearly two years.

1848.—THE PEOPLE'S ADVOCATE, AND NEW SOUTH WALES VINDICATOR. 16 pages.

Judging from appearance, this was a very respectable weekly newspaper. It advocated the extension of the franchise to the working classes, and lasted some four or five years. In 1851, Mr. Deniehy contributed to its columns. In the last edition of his History, Dr. Lang says, " The *People's Advocate* is a well-conducted paper, something more than Liberal in its politics, and very influential among the working classes."

1849.—THE AUSTRALIAN SPORTSMAN. 4 pages, illustrated.

No. 1, Saturday, 6th January, published weekly.

A very good sporting newspaper. The comic illustrations were well drawn, and the writing displayed a good deal of cleverness.

1850.—* The Freeman's Journal.

No. 1, June 30. Originally published twice a week, with eight pages, but on a change of proprietorship in 1865, it appeared as a weekly journal of twenty-four pages.

This paper was established as an organ of the Roman Catholic body, and was for many years exclusively religious. Until recently, it presented little to attract the general reader, and was quite devoid of talent in its editorial department. A year or two ago, however, its management passed into other hands, and its tone and appearance were immediately changed for the better. Mr. W. B. Dalley became a part proprietor, and contributed regularly to its columns. He was born in the Colony, in the year 1833, educated at St. Mary's College, and called to the Bar in 1856. The public mind was at that time deeply excited by the political changes which were taking place; Responsible Government was introduced for the first time; and amidst the electioneering struggles which agitated the country from one end to the other, the splendid oratorical powers possessed by Mr. Dalley were suddenly revealed. In democratical countries, eloquence, it is said, carries everything before it. The saying was certainly verified in the case of Mr. Dalley, and also, as will be shortly seen, in the case of another native of the Colony, Mr. Deniehy. These gentlemen were intimate associates, and were bound together, not alone by feelings of a personal nature, but by their appreciation of Literature. Both were endowed with the very highest capacities as public speakers, and both leaped at one bound—at almost the same moment—from the obscurity of private life into the sunshine of unbounded popularity. Mr. Dalley was a Member of the first Parliament under the new Constitution, and in November, 1858, was appointed Solicitor General. This office he retained for a few months only. It was accepted rather to suit the convenience of his colleagues than his own. Those members of the Bar who, by their seniority in the profession and position in public life, were most fitted to hold office, were in opposition to the gentlemen with whom Mr. Dalley was politically connected. The latter accordingly, with only two years' professional standing, was called upon to take office, and did so with reluctance. Soon after his resignation, he paid his first visit to England. In 1861, after his return to the Colony, he was appointed, in conjunction with Mr. Parkes, the present Colonial Secretary, a public lecturer, with a commission to lecture throughout the United Kingdom on the advantages offered by this country to emigrants. He returned in about twelve months, and sat for a short time in Parliament, but without taking any active interest in its proceedings. His practice at the Bar is very large, more especially in criminal cases. In all cases, indeed, in which an appeal to the jury is a matter of more than ordinary importance, he is invariably retained.

Mr. Dalley's writings, never of a sectarian character, are distinguished by their overflowing humour, sparkling imagery, and exquisite diction. Few can be more happy in their exercise of ridicule—a weapon which in most hands is used to wound, but not in his. So finely indeed is the bitterness of sarcasm tempered by the geniality of his humour, that even while engaged in political warfare, he has never made an enemy or estranged a friend. Fortunately, or unfortunately, he has withdrawn from political life, the asperities of which are foreign to his nature; and could we be certain that Literature would gain what has been lost to Politics, we should have infinite reason to rejoice.

The *Freeman's Journal* is now edited by Mr. Hutchinson, a graceful writer. Its circulation is about 1,600.

1850.—* THE EMPIRE.

No. 1. 28th December. Its first four issues were published weekly; it then appeared as a daily paper of six pages demy folio; then of four pages folio, and subsequently of eight.

This journal was commenced by Mr. Henry Parkes, in opposition to the *Herald*, and as the organ of what is sometimes termed the " Great Liberal Party " of the Colony. This party had at the time made itself extremely powerful by its agitation with respect to the Land Laws, and other leading topics of political interest ; and it was naturally supposed that a daily journal devoted to the exposition of their views would command very general favour. As one of the ablest and most consistent advocates of Liberalism, Mr. Parkes was well fitted to carry out the enterprise on which he had entered ; but journalism requires something more than political ability to make it successful. Although the *Empire* was well conducted by Mr. Parkes in its political and literary departments, it utterly failed in its commercial relations. After a severe struggle, the proprietor was obliged to yield to his misfortunes in the year 1858, and the *Empire* stopped. In May of the following year its publication was resumed under a new management, and it is now established as the second daily journal of the Colony. From its commencement the *Empire* has displayed a considerable amount of ability, and in that respect it may be favourably compared with its wealthier rival. Mr. Parkes is an able writer, and no one in the Colony is a better "thinker" on political matters. His speeches in Parliament display a higher capacity for dealing with the problems of Statecraft than those of any other man in it. It may be said that he, among all our politicians, makes the nearest approach to a Statesman. He is by no means a man of brilliant imagination, although he has published two volumes of poetry ; but, on the other hand, he is eminently clear and logical. He is now Colonial Secretary. He was editorially assisted, at different times, by Mr. James Martin, by Mr. Deniehy, and by Mr. Forster. On the revival of the *Empire* in 1859, Mr. Forster and Mr. Eagar were the principal contributors to its columns for some months. Mr. Eagar has been a very frequent contributor to the Press for many years back. He was born in the Colony, in 1818. A short memoir of him appeared in the *Southern Cross* of 1860, at the time when he was a Minister of the Crown in conjunction with his "school and form-fellow," Mr. Forster ; and from this memoir I extract the following :—

"During his business life (a period of five and twenty years), Mr. Eagar had acquired a high reputation for business ability ; but it is only known to a few personal friends that, during the whole of that period, Mr. Eagar found time, among his other active occupations, to contribute largely to the leading columns of the liberal Press. Long anterior to Responsible Government, and in the newspapers of the time—the *Monitor, Australian*, and *Examiner*— his writings, all in advocacy of liberal principles, are to be found. During the last ten years, he has contributed frequently, as a correspondent on political and financial subjects, to the *Sydney Morning Herald*, and also to the *Empire*, then under the proprietorship of Mr. Parkes. Among his later efforts in aid of the development of enlightened opinion, may be comprised the editorship of the *Church Sentinel*. To the *Empire*, under its present proprietorship, Mr. Eagar supplied numerous leading articles on the chief subjects of political interest, from June to October of last year."

Mr. Eagar is now, for the third time, a Minister of the Crown.

One of the present editors of the *Empire* is Mr. William Wilkes. Previous to his connection with this journal, he was editor of the Brisbane *Courier*, and occupied that position for eight years—from 1848 to 1856. He earned a considerable reputation in Brisbane by his humourous writings—a reputation which still survives in that city, after an absence of many years. Long before he was connected with any journal—before, in fact, there was any journal in Brisbane to be connected with—he displayed his talent as an impromptu humourist while living in the bush. Amusing sketches, hastily written on a desk composed of a piece of bark, were handed about from friend to friend, till copies were multiplied, and the author's name become a synonyme

E

for humour. In 1856, he came to Sydney, and contributed to several periodicals which no longer exist. In the *Month* he wrote a clever *novelette*, entitled "Charles Wotton, or Bush Life in Australia." On the re-establishment of the *Empire* in 1859, he joined its staff in an editorial capacity. As a political writer he is not excelled by any one, of the present day, in this Colony; and his contributions to the *Empire* constitute much of that journal's value. Although produced with little labour, and less premeditation, they are neither shallow nor injudicious; but are invariably distinguished by good taste, accurate thinking, and abundant humour.

Mr. J. J. Harpur wrote many articles in this journal some time ago. Mr. Bennett, one of the proprietors, is also an occasional contributor to its columns. He is the author of an excellent "History of Australian Discovery and Colonisation," now in course of publication. Another contributor is the Rev. Mr. Ridley, whose treatises on the Language of the Aboriginals are noticed in a subsequent page.

The circulation of the *Empire* is generally stated to be about half the circulation of the *Herald*. Besides the daily issue, a *Weekly Empire* is also published, for distribution in the interior.

1851.—THE PRESS.

No. 1, October. Published weekly.

A third periodical commenced by the indefatigable Dr. Lang. It was ably written during the short term of its existence—a term which did not extend beyond a few months. Dr. Lang paid a visit to England, and the *Press* ceased on his departure from the Colony.

1852.—The Courier.

This publication seems to have disappeared altogether. The only trace of it I can find is in Dr. Lang's History, where it is stated that " The *Courier* has been recently started by the publicans of Sydney, who of course all take it in."

1853.—The Australian Witness.

The contents of this periodical, which lasted a year or two, were principally of a religious character.

1853.—The Illustrated Sydney News. 8 pages. Price, 6d. No. 1, October 9. Published weekly.

The earlier numbers of this periodical shew little excellence, either artistic or literary ; but in the second year of its existence, a considerable improvement is manifest in its appearance. It was enlarged in size from 8 to 16 pages. It was unfortunate in its artists, however, at all times; but it possessed an excellent engraver in Mr. Mason, formerly of the *Illustrated London New*. Its letter-press is remarkable rather for carefulness in the selection of extracts than for the originality of its contributions. No. 53 affords some information with respect to its position at that time :—" The *Illustrated Sydney News* prints 4,000 copies of its new series, and contains six pages of advertisements, reserving its remaining ten pages for the double purposes of a weekly newspaper (adapted for the city and the bush), and the attractions of pictorial illustration. We possess, therefore, a larger circulation than is boasted by any weekly publication in the Colony, and take place, in this respect, next to the daily journals of Sydney. Our circulation is increasing in the sister Colonies, in America, and in India ; and the number of our English subscribers (by no means inconsiderable) is augmenting rapidly. We have admitted unreservedly that hitherto our periodical has not taken a foremost rank. It has, from the very novelty of the undertaking, had to struggle with existence. Feebleness in its literary department, haste in the pictorial, and irregularity in the despatching of the paper, were unavoidably attendant on such a condition. We trust, for the future, to be enabled to give our illustrations more time and finish, and to improve materially upon their style and character. We have added to our staff of artists and engravers very valuable reinforcements. We have secured the pen of one who has succeeded in dealing powerfully with public topics ; and for the magazine department of our paper, its proper aid. We trust that scientific writers will also be attracted to our columns."

These efforts, however, were unavailing, and the publication sank, in its third year of existence, involving a heavy loss to its proprietors. A large number of its illustrations were republished in 1859, with a preface by Mr. Fowler, under the title of *The Australian Picture Pleasure Book.*

1855.—The Illustrated Sydney Journal: *a Weekly Record of News, Science, Literature, and Art.* 12 pages, 4to. Price, 6d.

No. 1, July 14. The illustrations in this publication are not of a high order in art, but they are very fair. The letter-press consists principally of the usual light reading—tales, extracts, and witticisms.

1855.—The Sydney Sketch-book.

Published weekly.

The editor of this periodical was Mr. H. E. Watts, a writer of more than ordinary powers. He excelled in sarcasm and humour. The *Sketch Book* was in the nature of a *Punch ;* but, although it was remarkably well written, it did not live long. Mr. Watts was for some time a contributor to the *Herald*, under the signature "Quill." He subsequently went to Melbourne, where he became editor of the *Argus.*

1856.—A German newspaper was printed in this year.

1856.—SYDNEY PUNCH.

Published weekly.

This publication presented little attraction to the public. It was very deficient in talent, both artistic and literary, and its existence was limited to a few months.

1856.—THE CHURCH OF ENGLAND CHRONICLE.

No. 1, Saturday, October 1. Published twice a month, subsequently enlarged, and published once a month.

A religious publication.

1857.—SYDNEY PUNCH.

The editor of this paper was Mr. Wilkes, already mentioned, and among its contributors were Mr. Sealy and Mr. Rowe— "Menippus" and "Peter 'Possum." Each of these gentlemen possessed marked talent for humour, though each of a different kind. Mr. Wilkes is a master of the art of "squibbery." His compositions take the form of prose, and are produced with great ease and rapidity. Mr. Sealy, on the other hand, to adopt a vulgar phrase, "cultivated the Muse." No one could exert his powers of ridicule more gracefully than he did. The volume he has left behind contains abundant proofs of his capacity as a satirist. Mr. Rowe contributed an article to the *Month*, entitled "A Bather's Mishap," which displays remarkable humour; it would do credit to any periodical in London. The periodical in Sydney, however, to which these gentlemen contributed, was cut off at a very early period of its career; it expired with its fourth issue. Singular to relate, the cause of its extinction was precisely the reverse of that which usually brings about the ruin of literary enterprise. One of its proprietors suddenly found himself in possession of unexpected wealth, and apparently preferring his ease to his literary dignity, he immediately abandoned *Punch*, leaving its talented editor in the lurch.

1857.—The Australian Banner. 8 pages.

No. 1, January. Published weekly.

A religious publication.

1857.—The Era.

A sporting journal, published weekly, and intended to compete with *Bell's Life in Sydney*. Mr. Wilkes was a contributor, but not on sporting topics. It lasted a year or so.

1858.—Sydney Dispatch: *a Weekly Journal of Politics, Commerce, and Literature*. 12 pages.

No. 1, Saturday 3 July. This was "the first Australian journal printed entirely with colonial-made type." The type was cast in Sydney; and certainly, no paper could be better printed than the *Dispatch*. Mr. Wilkes was among its contributors for a short period.

1858.—The Church Sentinel.

No. 1, November.

A religious publication, stated to have been "started by a few Members of the Anglican Laity, to resist a threatened Episcopal despotism." It also contended for the abolition of State Aid to Religion—a policy which has been recently carried into effect. The *Sentinel* (which did not live long) was edited by Mr. Geoffrey Eagar, the present Colonial Treasurer. Mr. William Forster also wrote for it.

1858.—The Spectator.

This publication, which appeared once a fortnight, was a curiosity, having been "edited by au Association of Ladies," at the head of which was a Mrs. Cora Anna Weekes, who had recently arrived from California. Its first number appeared in July, and its last followed soon after.

1859.—The Sydney Evening Mail. 4 pages.

The first attempt in the Colony to establish an evening paper. It lasted some three or four months only. Its publication began in February, and ceased in May, on the re-appearance of the daily *Empire*.

1859.—The Southern Cross: *a Weekly Journal of Politics, Literature, and Social Progress.* 16 pages.

No. 1, October 1.

Several contributions, both in verse and prose, from the pen of the celebrated R. H. Horne, appeared in this journal. They were sent by him from the Blue Mountains, in Victoria, to the editor, for whom he entertained strong feelings of friendship. This editor was Daniel Henry Denichy—in many respects the most brilliant man that this country has produced. He was born in Sydney, on the 18th August, 1828, and he died at Bathurst, on the 22nd October, 1865, in the thirty-eighth year of his age. When a child, he went with his parents to England, and resided there for a short time. He received his education in his native place, and that education was simply a school one. In his youth he was articled to Mr. Stenhouse, an attorney, and in due time was admitted to practice. Mr. Stenhouse is a gentleman who has cultivated Literature throughout his life, and who has distinguished himself by the ardent interest he has displayed in all matters connected with it. His library is one of the largest private collections in the Colony, numbering many thousands of volumes of classical and European literature. It was while pursuing his studies under the care of this accomplished gentleman, that Mr. Deniehy first gave signs of that intellectual power for which he was afterwards so distinguished. With very slight advantages in his favour, he contrived to make himself master of almost the whole field of European Literature—to attain a thorough insight into the various developments of Art—and to qualify himself for the most marked displays of talent, both as a politician and a man of letters. The extent and accuracy of his attainments were astonishing. He seemed to possess a peculiar faculty for making himself familiar with every subject that attracted his attention. He penetrated by the mere force of genius into things which to most men are mysteries, requiring an apprenticeship to understand. In the domain of Literature he was probably without an equal in this country, in his power of conception as well as in the range of his acquisitions. His mind was essentially original and creative. He has not, unfortunately, left much behind him that can be pointed to in evidence of this assertion; but the little that does remain is quite sufficient to prove it.

The brilliancy and power of his intellect were not publicly manifested until circumstances had made him a public character. The political struggles which attended the introduction of Parliamentary Government in 1856 afforded him many opportunities of displaying the great oratorical powers which nature, in addition to her other gifts, had bestowed upon him. Rarely have greater triumphs been achieved by any public speaker in this Colony than those which were achieved by Mr. Denichy. He was returned to Parliament in 1857, and again in the two succeeding years. While in the Assembly he was a vigorous opponent of the Cowper Ministry—a Ministry which had been formed under the auspices of Liberalism, of which he himself was an ardent advocate. It may be doubted whether the influence of politics upon Literature has ever been a salutary one. It cannot be doubted that Mr. Denichy, like many other brilliant men of letters, suffered from his devotion to political interests. He was drawn away from his proper field, his mind was embittered by factious struggles, and those powers, which might otherwise have been concentrated on a work of genius, were frittered away in the pursuit of some immediate object. When he was no longer a Member of the

Assembly, he was instrumental in establishing the *Southern Cross*, which, so long as it existed, unceasingly and bitterly opposed Mr. Cowper and his friends. His contributions to it, forming nearly the whole of its original matter, at once gave it a high character, both as a literary and a political journal. It was decidedly one of the very ablest journals we have seen in Sydney. The critical notices written by the editor afford striking evidence of his power as a critic—a power, indeed, which was altogether of the highest quality. In political satire his weapon was of the most trenchant character. A piece of this description, entitled " How I became Attorney General of New Barataria," ridiculing the manner in which the most important offices in the State had been filled up, is not only the most brilliant political satire written in this Colony, but one of the most brilliant in the English language. It would have gained its author the hearty admiration of the men who sat round Mr. Fraser's dinner-table some thirty or forty years ago ; but, as it was, it estranged from him some of his best and most valuable friends. On the termination of the *Southern Cross*, in less than a year after its first number had appeared, Mr. Deniehy left this Colony for Melbourne. He there edited, for about two years, a weekly journal called the *Victorian*, in the interests of the Roman Catholic party. He returned to Sydney in 1864, but his health had failed, and his mental power was almost extinguished.

The following tribute to his memory was paid by his illustrious friend, Mr. R. H. Horne, in the columns of a Melbourne journal. No one, perhaps, was better qualified to estimate his intellectual worth ; and the language in which this estimate is expressed, will sufficiently shew that there is no exaggeration in what has been said of him above :—

" A telegram from Sydney informs us of a loss which many in New South Wales, and not a few in other places, will feel deeply, and not the less so because it has long been foreseen to be as inevitable as irreparable. Last

Sunday night, Mr. D. H. Deniehy, once the eloquent, the witty, the erudite, and vigorous leader of the Opposition in the Parliament of New South Wales, and well known for the extraordinary extent of his reading, fell senseless in the streets of Bathurst, and was carried to the hospital, where he died before daybreak on Monday morning.

"The fate of an American celebrity, whose genius and writings Mr. Deniehy so much admired (Edgar Allan Poe), had often been predicted with regard to himself, and indeed it required a very slight degree of the prophetic seer to know that the fate could scarcely, in the end, be otherwise. For years past it had become quite evident that life had lost all its natural charms for him, and that if he did not directly court Death, he at least set the 'grisly terror' at defiance, or treated the frequent approach with scornful indifference. A few words may serve to explain the cause of this. Mr. Deniehy had, as a young man, worked very hard and unceasingly, perhaps to an injurious extent, during fifteen or sixteen years; he then burst forth a youthful meteor upon the quiet atmosphere of Sydney, first by the brilliant eloquence of his lectures on poetry and literature—English, French, and Italian; and next as a political orator. He was at once recognised and hailed as the first and brightest genius of Australian growth. Every fresh effort met with unmingled applause. He was a remarkable instance of an immediate success in life. Without passing through any of the intermediate gradations of failures, mortifications, and bitter disappointments, he sprang at once, or rather was at once placed upon the apex of contemporaneous fame; he stood upon the 'topmost round of Fortune's wheel,' and it was too much even for his strong brain to bear without becoming giddy and toppling over. Perhaps it would have been too much for any young brain; but such a success is so very rare, indeed almost unique, that the pen that would reprehend his fall may do wisely to pause first, and consider the overwhelming nature of the circumstances. Let it be here conceded that the above is only an individual elucidation; other causes may also have been at work.

"D. H. Deniehy, among all young men of Australian birth (and we might put the statement in a far wider form), was the brightest spirit, the most elaborate of general readers, the largest of scope as to intellectual sympathies; one of the most varied in attainments, with respect to a knowledge of the best and most *recherché* books in both ancient and modern languages, the cryptic and archaic being to him as familiar as the merely elegant or evanescent; and this applies no less to the knowledge he had of pictures, architecture, sculpture, and articles of *vertu*. In addition to this, he possessed a wonderful memory, and was gifted, beyond all other 'sons of the soil,' with ready wit and genuine eloquence. These latter qualities with him were no mere clap-traps to serve for momentary effects—he had the thoughts that uplift, and the 'words that burn.'

"The feeling for abstract idealistic beauty appeared in Mr. Deniehy to be almost an additional sense; he seemed actually to taste the beautiful; his mouth watered at words as if they were peaches; he appeared to have a sensuous impression of the ideal, with such fullness and force did his imagination realize a graphic thought; and yet he had so well-stored and practical an intellect and understanding, and so keen and subtle a knowledge of men and things, that he might have risen to the highest positions in the Government of New South Wales, but for the corrosive influence of one evil among all his great gifts and good fortunes. No man, perhaps, ever had a larger number of personal friends—friends who were devoted to him, and from whom any money, any kindness, any service could be obtained, and generally without asking; but he had one fatal enemy—an enemy unceasing and remorseless—through the whole day, and through the whole night pursuing him even in his dreams. He would speak of this himself, at times, and in a most learned, and no less cunning way, to disarm and cut the ground from under his hearer, and give, as a psychological reason why it was not of the least use for him even to make any effort to master his accursed foe, that he was a victim to 'the fatal paralysis of the will.' It was therefore illogical and unphilosophical for anybody to offer him any advice. No man, for any essential purpose, could help another man, &c.

"This is not a time to enter upon any detailed outlines of his brief career. It was brief indeed as to the too much light, and all the sad remainder was a grim and phantasmal nightmare, surpassing all experience and all belief. Peace be to his wasted and wandering genius, and may all those forms of loveliness and refined grace on which he most delighted to discourse, hover over him, and infuse their spirit through his now unbroken sleep! Those who knew him in his better hours will join in this prayer; and those who only knew him otherwise may forgive this poor white stone now laid with mournful memories upon his untimely grave.

"The subject of this too hasty sketch has left very little to justify what has been here said of him; but all those who intimately knew him will be well aware how true it is. Instead of a small local circle, here and there, he might have had an extensive reputation, and taken rank as one of the most marked men for colonial history up to the present time. As it is, he has only left a few essays, sketches, stray papers, and journalistic waifs, and a number of admirable private letters,—'the rest is silence.' "

Another competent critic, who, in former years, was an intimate friend of Mr. Deniehy, expressed his opinion of the intellectual qualities of the latter on the same occasion. This was Mr. Dalley. The following article from his pen appeared in the *Freeman's Journal* :—

"In a remote town of the interior, away from family and friends, died suddenly, in the 33rd year of his age, on Sunday, 22nd instant, Daniel Henry Deniehy. His death demands more than a passing notice from all who respect great talents, and admire high intellectual culture. Mr. Deniehy may justly be regarded as the most brilliant of the native-born inhabitants of this country. Of rare natural abilities, his youth was marked by an earnest and impassioned love of Literature. At a period of life when with most of us the real business of education is only commencing, he had collected and arranged the treasures of rich and varied scholarship. Many will recollect the child-like face and delicate figure of the boy lecturer of ten or fifteen years ago upon the platform of literary assemblages, holding large audiences entranced with the magic of his eloquence, and inspiring not less admiration of his genius than wonder at the precocity of his talents. An unrivalled orator by nature, as well as by careful cultivation, he devoted the early years of his brief manhood to the instruction and elevation of his young countrymen. He successively treated the Literatures of Rome, of France, of Italy, and of England ; and it is not too much to assert that, in this country, at all events, no such admirable discourses were ever pronounced. In the midst of the enthusiasm excited by his genius, he was invited to contest the electorate of Argyle, in which he was then resident, as a candidate for its representation in Parliament. His speech upon the hustings on this occasion was a model of public oratory. Victorious in this struggle, he entered Parliament with the highest reputation, and the most unclouded prospects of honor and distinction. Meanwhile he was known as a contributor to the Press of the Colony, of many articles in prose and verse, of rare excellence. As a

Member of the Legislature, his career was not marked by the splendid success which all who knew him anticipated as the reward of his ability. It may be urged, in explanation of this disappointment, that he had few sympathies in common with the majority of those with whom he became politically associated, and that his nature was not sufficiently yielding to accommodate itself to the compromises of his party. He, however, took a conspicuous position in Parliament on all great occasions, and was uniformly listened to with a respectful attention rarely accorded to others. The intensity of his convictions, and the irritability produced by extreme physical feebleness, placed him in antagonism to many who would have preferred his friendship to his hostility. It was his misfortune that he was unable to recognize the possibility of continuing friendships originating in agreement of opinion upon public questions, beyond the period of the maintenance of such political accord. To the deep regret of his friends, he alienated himself from most of those with whom he had entered public life, and identified himself in the discussion of public questions. An unrivalled master of sarcasm—he employed his talents to widen impassably the breach between his former allies and himself. We abstain from pronouncing any opinion upon the justice and propriety of his course of action. His rules for the government of his own public conduct were rigorous to the last degree; and he inexorably required of others what he himself laboriously endeavoured to exhibit in his own person—the highest consistency of conduct. Looking down upon his grave, which holds so much that was once so loved and admired, and from which so many of the fruits of a great and honorable life were expected, his survivors will forget the bitterness of his hostility, and only remember the former triumphs of his noble intellect, ere sorrow, and infirmity, and disappointment, had clouded, weakened, and broken his genius. Few will think of the luminous spirit now gone from our midst, without a tear of regret for so much power lost for ever, and of pity for a life which gave such promise of greatness, and went out in suffering, in poverty, and bitter mental distress."

Allusion has been made to the extraordinary variety of Mr. Deniehy's attainments, and to his faculty for accumulating information on subjects to which he might have been supposed a stranger. The following testimony was supplied by a correspondent to a local paper soon after Mr. Deniehy's death :—

"Sir,—May I be permitted, through your journal, to pay a passing tribute to the memory of the late Daniel Henry Deniehy? Your cotemporary has touched upon his history with a tender and a loving hand; I should wish to do so in the same spirit. Known only to me through his public life, I have never possessed the privilege of that familiar intercourse which seems to have charmed all who enjoyed it. On one occasion, and one only, had I the pleasure of making his acquaintance, and the impression produced upon me by his extraordinary intellect was such that I have never forgotten it, and most probably never shall. We were once weather-bound travellers at a solitary way-side inn, and, of course, thrown a good deal on each other's society for amusement. I soon discovered I was in the presence of no ordinary man, and indulged, as you may suppose, in many conjectures as to who this extraordinary talker could be. However, I was not long in the dark, for in the evening he grew communicative, and drawing his chair up to the fire, he indulged in a thoroughly Coleridgean monologue, I all the while, to borrow Carlyle's words, sitting 'a passive bucket to be pumped into'—and very contented was I to be so. I cannot say now whether it was the eloquence of his language, or the vast stores of his knowledge, which attracted me most; but between the two, I was spell-bound. In the course of the second evening we were joined by another visitor. I know not who he was, but he was an artist, or some one intimately acquainted with Art in all its branches. Mr. Deniehy was soon in conversation with this gentleman on the contents of the different Continental Galleries. With those of Dresden and Munich he appeared to be perfectly familiar, and you would have thought he carried a catalogue of the Louvre collection in his pocket. Presently the conversation changed to engraving, which I could see was rather a *spécialité* of our new friend. But here Mr. Deniehy was equally at home; and I remember his specifying particular engravings at the Louvre, as illustrative of various styles, or various processes in the art. He afterwards gave us a minute history of silhouette portraiture. Now, considering silhouette has been 'out' for years, one might almost say for centuries, we may well wonder at his familiarity with such an out of the way subject. He has always seemed to me to resemble De Quincey. They were alike in person—both mere tenements for the spirit within; alike in the copiousness of their information, in their eloquence and precision of style, in their irregular and unrestrained efforts; alike, too, in their frequent pilgrimages to that dreamland, that enchanted realm, that faery ground of imagination, which has ever been a lure and a snare to the best and wisest of us. Peace be to his ashes!"

A similar memorial appeared iu another local paper, at a later date. It was addressed from the Murrumbidgee River. After alluding to Mr. Deniehy's schoolboy days at the old Sydney College, the writer went on to say :—

"After he left school, which he was obliged to do early, in consequence of declining health, I lost sight of him till I met him in Goulburn in 1854. Many who read this will recall the delight he gave on one occasion by a lecture on Scotch Poetry. The Court House was crowded, and for two hours his audience remained in rapt attention, listening to the torrent which, without check or hindrance, poured from his eloquent lips. His quotations were all from memory, all his notes being contained on half a sheet of paper. After that lecture I retired with him to his lodgings, and he kept me while he continued on the subject for nearly two hours more. His memory was something marvellous. I have sometimes thought he had read every book worth reading that was ever printed, and I do verily believe that nothing which he ever read was forgotten. He had travelled over the whole field of English Literature, was a very respectable classic, and was well acquainted with the modern languages, speaking French fluently. His greatest oratorical triumphs were achieved at political meetings. The effect of his first speech at the Circular Quay, in Sydney, will never be forgotten by those who heard it. Some of his best speeches were delivered in Goulburn, among which I may especially mention that on the occasion of his election, in February, 1857 * * * His end was sad—terribly sad. Always weakly, his unwearied industry, his severe and unremitting brain work, reduced him to such a state of physical exhaustion that he found relief only when under the influence of artificial stimulants. And therefore he sought them again, and yet again he sought them, and the end of all is to be found in the simple grave at Bathurst a stranger's kindness has provided for him. He could not have been more than thirty-six * * * As I cast this poor wreath on his grave, I cannot but feel with Burke, that 'I live in an inverted order,' and can only again lament over poor, gifted, lost Deniehy."

1860.—* THE SYDNEY MAIL. 8 pages, subsequently 12.

No. 1, 7 July. Published weekly.

This is a weekly issue from the *Herald* office, containing the news of the week, with a variety of extracts and original articles.

Its circulation is principally in the country. At its first appearance it contaiued 8 pages, and had about 2,000 subscribers. In 1863 it was enlarged to 12 pages, and its circulation was then over 8,000. This has now increased to 11,500.

1860.—* THE WEEKLY EMPIRE.

A similar publication to the foregoing.

1862.—THE INDEX. 8 pages, 4to.

No. 1, Saturday, 18th October. Published weekly.

The editor, proprietor, printer, and publisher of this periodical was a person styling himself "The Honorable William Radley." The publication apparently originated in a desire to bring himself into public notice, to publish his own private grievances, and to attack the order of Freemasonry. After the issue of a few numbers, the office of the *Index* was burned to the ground, and the honorable proprietor made a precipitate retreat from the Colony. He was subsequently captured by the police, and brought to trial ou the charge of arson. The trial resulted in a rather severe sentence.

1863.—THE CORNSTALK.

A small weekly paper, the contents of which consisted of original tales (written principally by the editor, Mr. Whitworth), answers to correspondents, receipts for puddings, original poetry, and conundrums. It lived for a few months only. Mr. Whitworth has been connected with several Australian journals as a reporter, and is a very ready writer. He has recently edited a valuable work of reference—*Baillière's Gazetteer for New South Wales.*

1864.—THE COMMERCIAL TIMES OF NEW SOUTH WALES : *a record of Mercantile News, Shipping Intelligence, Mining Transactions, Prices Current, &c., &c.* Conducted by Cyril Cecil. 10 pages.

No. 1, Saturday, 5th March. Published weekly.

1864.—THE SYDNEY TIMES : *A Journal for the promotion of Australian Literature, and the advocacy of encouragement to Native Industry.* 8 pages.

No. 1, April 2. Published weekly.

This publication owed its origin to the " Protectionists," a class which, at the time of its appearance, was engaged in strenuous efforts to convert the Legislature to its views. It was edited by Mr. J. J. Harpur, a brother of the Poet, whose labours as a journalist have extended over many years ; and its pages contain several contributions from Mr. Charles Harpur, and from Mr. Dalley. Although encouraged by many wealthy politicians, the *Times* died at the end of its first quarter.

1864.—* SYDNEY PUNCH. 16 pages, 4to.

No. 1, Friday, 27th May. Published weekly.

This is the only attempt to establish a humourous periodical in the Colony, which has met with any degree of success. It is a superior production to its predecessors, more especially in its drawings. Some of these are extremely good. The first artist attached to it was Mr. E. J. Greig, formerly of Melbourne. He was a young man of considerable genius, with an enthusiastic love for his profession. His merit was the greater in that he was entirely self-taught. Had his life been spared, he would un-doubtedly have attained, in the maturity of his powers, a high degree of excellence. Unfortunately, however, a few months after he had begun his work, he was drowned in the harbour, with every member of his family, by the upsetting of a boat in a

F

sudden squall. His place is now occupied by Mr. M. Scott, whose talent as an artist, though of a different order from that of Mr. Greig, is justly admired. The literary merit of this periodical has generally been acknowledged. Considering the difficulties under which it has laboured—not the least among which, is the difficulty of procuring a sufficient number of contributors—it is fully entitled to whatever praise has been awarded it. Some of its early numbers contained pieces of remarkable merit from the pen of Mr. J. B. Stiffe, a gentleman who was formerly a contributor to several periodicals in London, and who is now editor of the Melbourne *Punch*. He is an accomplished manufacturer of jokes. Mr. W. B. Dalley, the brightest intellect among us, has contributed largely to its columns. His talent as a humourist is very great, while his style is remarkable for purity and grace of language. Mr. Deniehy also wrote for it during the last year of his life, but his power had then gone from him. Many contributions from the pen of Mr. Hutchinson have possessed merit. Latterly, *Punch* has been edited by Mr. G. R. Morton, of whom mention has already been made. In what is called " broad humour," he is not surpassed by any writer in the Colony. He is deficient, however, like most of our writers, in constructive power, and his wit is consequently limited in its range. The circulation of this periodical does not exceed 1,000.

1864.—* The Illustrated Sydney News. 16 pages. Price, 6d. No. 1, Thursday, June 16. Published monthly.

This publication presents a far more attractive appearance than its predecessor of 1853. The illustrations are very good, and the printing could not be better. It is still in existence, and promises to become permanent. The circulation during the first five months is stated to have averaged 6,000 copies a month. Up to the present time it has averaged over 8,500. It is published in time for the English Mail every month, and a large number of copies are thus disposed of.

1865.—THE CHURCH CHRONICLE. 14 pages, 4to.

1865.—* THE CHRISTIAN PLEADER: *a Journal of General Religious Intelligence.* 14 pages, 4to.

1866.—* THE ILLUSTRATED SPORTING LIFE AND PASTORAL REGISTER. 4 pages.
No. 1, 28th July. Published weekly.

This is the last of several attempts to drive *Bell's Life* out of the field. It is at present published without illustrations, and under the title of *The Sydney Sporting Life.*

1866.—* THE TEMPERANCE ADVOCATE.
No. 1, Saturday, 8th September. Published twice a month.

The following is a list of Country Newspapers now in circulation. With one or two exceptions, they are well printed and well conducted :—

Albury Banner.
Armidale Express.
Bathurst Free Press.
   ,,   Times.
Bega Gazette.
Braidwood Dispatch.
Border Post.
Clarence River Examiner.
Deniliquin Chronicle.
Dubbo Dispatch.
Golden Age.
Goulburn Chronicle and Herald.
   ,,   Argus.
Illawarra Mercury.
   ,,   Express.
   ,,   Times.
Kiama Independent.
Lachlan Reporter.
Macleay Herald.
Maitland Mercury.*

Maitland Ensign.
Monaro Mercury.
   ,,   Star.
Morpeth Leader.
Moruya Examiner.
Mudgee Liberal.
Murrumbidgee Herald.
Newcastle Chronicle.
   ,,   Standard.
Pastoral Times.
Riverine Herald.
Singleton Times.
Tamworth Examiner.
Tenterfield Chronicle.
Tumut and Adelong Times.
Wagga Wagga Express.
Western Examiner.
Western Post.
Yass Courier.

* The circulation of the *Maitland Mercury*, which is published three times a week, is about 9,000 weekly.

II.—MAGAZINES.

1821.—The Australian Magazine : *a Compendium of Religious, Literary, and Miscellaneous Intelligence.*

No. 1, May 1. Published monthly. 32 pages, 8vo. Price, 1s. 3d.

This was the first magazine published in the Colony. The contents of the first number are as follows :—(1) Extract of a Letter from Governor Macquarie, giving his "sanction and approbation" to the magazine ; (2) A Life of the eminent Missionary, Swartz ; (3) A Sermon on the truth, importance, and design of Revelation ; (4) History of Water Snakes, Sea Snakes, and Sea Serpents ; (5) "On Liberality of Sentiment"; (6) Letter to the Editor ; (7) Allegory on Impudence and Modesty ; (8) Literary Intelligence ; (9) Religious Intelligence ; (10) General Information ; (11) Agricultural Report ; (12) Select Poetry.

The appearance of this magazine is by no means good, the paper and type being of a very inferior description. It was printed by George Howe, the publisher of the *Sydney Gazette;* and it seems that, up to the year 1821, no other printing office had been established in the Colony. The thirteenth number contains an announcement that the magazine would appear, after that issue, as a quarterly, instead of a monthly, publication ; the reason assigned being the want of mechanical facilities. The publisher hints at the expected receipt of a " liberal and diversified supply of type" from Europe, which would enable him to overcome the difficulties in his way.

The contents of the *Australian Magazine* display no talent. They are principally of a religious character, suggesting the idea that the editor was a clergyman, and that he was under the necessity of writing the whole of the magazine himself. At a much later period, we find the failure of many similar publications ascribed to the difficulty of finding contributors ; the editor being, in most cases, left to furnish the contents with his own pen.

1827.—THE SOUTH ASIAN REGISTER.

90 pages, 8vo.

The contents of the fourth number are as follows :—(1) " New Holland," a description of the Colony ; (2) Review of a work entitled " The Campaigns of the British Army in America"; (3) " Walk through Sydney in 1828," a lively sketch of the city as it appeared then ; (4) " A Now, descriptive of a hot day in England," an amusing article taken from Leigh Hunt's *Indicator ;* (5) " Missions"; (6) Verse, " Blighted Hope"; (7) " Philology and the South Sea Islands"; (8) " The Register," containing lists of prices, and other similar information.

Copies of these old periodicals are extremely rare ; in fact, it is sometimes difficult to procure even a single number. The only copy of the *South Asian* which I can meet with, is bound up in a volume of " Pamphlets" belonging to the Australian Library.

The editor was a Dr. Oldfield, whose fame has not survived his publication. The *Register* appears to have been an interesting Miscellany of average merit. A paragraph on " Colonial Literature," in the fourth number, published in December, contains the following :—" Since the commencement of this journal, two others have made their appearance in Sydney, published quarterly or so ; the first edited by the Rev. C. P. N. Wilton, and the second by Mr. Fulton, *an Australian.* Of their merits or demerits we have no wish to speak, especially as both publications are considered to be now defunct. We feel pleased, however, by observing the indulgence which they, along with ourselves, have met from the public of this infant community." In the same number it is said, that " The man of literature in Sydney can speculate on no rank with probability, beyond that of the scrivener or the pedagogue."

1828.—MURRAY'S AUSTRAL-ASIATIC REVIEW.

100 pages.   Price, 5s.

A publication under the above title was announced to appear
on the 1st of January, 1828, but it is impossible to say whether
it appeared or not, as no copy of it can be found.

1828.—THE AUSTRALIAN QUARTERLY JOURNAL OF THEOLOGY,
LITERATURE, AND SCIENCE : Edited by the Rev. C. P. N.
Wilton, M.A., *Fellow of the Cambridge Philosophical Society,
late Scholar of St. John's College, Cambridge, Master of the
King's Female Orphan Institution, Parramatta, and one of His
Majesty's Assistant Chaplains in the Colony of New South Wales.*

No. 1, January, 112 pages.   Price, 5s.

This is a far more imposing publication than its predecessors.
The contents of the first number are—(1) Introduction ; (2)
" Article on the connection between Religion and Science"; (3)
Sermon by the Editor, on "The Beauty of Order in the Church of
England"; (4) A Funeral Hymn ; (5) Reviews of new publica-
tions ; (6) Verses on "The Deluge," "The New Year"; (7)
Suggestions for the establishment of an Australian Museum ; (8)
The late Tour of Mr. A. Cunningham ; (9) Humourous verses,
"The Mineralogist"; (10) Australian Sperm Whale Fishery; (11)
The Agricultural and Horticultural Society of New South Wales ;
(12) Remarks on Saxon Sheep-farming ; (13) Visitation of the
Archdeacon ; (14) State of the Colony.

So far as type and paper are concerned, this periodical
presents a respectable appearance ; but it seems that the editor
had to contend with the same mechanical difficulties that beset
the path of his predecessor.   No. II contains an apology to the
reader for making its appearance two months behind time ; the
reason alleged being " certain circumstances connected with the
Press."   As regards its literary merits, there is an evident

sameness in the contents, betraying a lack of contributors; but otherwise it is a creditable production. The first number was savagely reviewed in the *Monitor*, principally on account of some supercilious remarks made by Mr. Wilton, in his notice of Threlkeld's work on the Aboriginal Dialects.

1833.—THE NEW SOUTH WALES MAGAZINE.

No. 1, August. Published monthly. 63 pages. Price, 2s. 6d.

The contents of the second number are—(1) Introductory discourse delivered at the opening of the Sydney Mechanics' School of Arts, April 23, 1833, by the Rev. H. Carmichael, A.M., Vice-President of that Institution; (2) Verse by Henry Halloran, on "Australian Scenery—Coodgee"; (3) Article on "Moreton Bay and Port Bowen"; (4) Retribution of the Aborigines; (5) Proposed Improvements iu Sydney; (6) Review of "Mr. Busby's Publications"; (7) Verse on "The Beauties of England," "written in the Bush of New South Wales"; (8) The Transportation System; (9) The Pythoness, a Tale of the First Century, written for the *New South Wales Magazine*, by Mythos; (10) Natural History Department, conducted by Dr. John Lhotsky; Australian Zoology, by the editor; (11) Historical Register, containing political and general information relating to the affairs of the Colony.

The editor and proprietor of this magazine was the Rev. Ralph Mansfield, already mentioned. There is not much vivacity in the contents of its pages, but it adequately represented the literary condition of the time. In the preface to the first volume, the editor says: "In reviewiug its pages, we are far from feeling that all has been done which the resources of the Colony, the talents of our contributors, or our own individual exertions, might have rendered practicable. The plan originally laid down in our prospectus has been very imperfectly accomplished—not from any unforeseen want of materials, for they have proved even more copious than we could have anticipated, nor yet from want of diligence on our part. The publication was undertaken as an experiment—and as an experiment from which many would have been deterred by the fate of previous trials. Several works of a similar character were started, at different times, some years ago; but it was found that the reading public was then too scanty to afford them adequate support, and they were soon discontinued. It was therefore necessary, in renewing the attempt, to proceed cautiously—not merely for the sake of our own interests, but from the consideration that another failure would be discreditable to the Colony, and retard, for many years, its advancement in periodical literature."

1835.—ILLUSTRATIONS OF THE PRESENT STATE AND FUTURE PROSPECTS OF THE COLONY OF NEW SOUTH WALES. By an Impartial Observer.

34 pages.

NEW SOUTH WALES LITERARY, POLITICAL, AND COMMERCIAL ADVERTISER.

16 pages.

Under these titles, an eccentric personage, named Dr. Lhotsky, endeavoured to establish a monthly periodical—the *Illustrations* and the *Advertiser* forming two parts of one design. In the latter he states: "The advertising public is respectfully informed that the above publication is the only one in the shape of a Review or Magazine existing in this Colony, whereas Van Diemen's Land possesses two periodicals of this kind." The design was a failure. It apparently originated in "the entire inattention of the Government of New South Wales to my geographical discoveries and collections of natural history." Dr. Lhotsky had some pretensions to scientific attainments, and was the author of a *Journey to the Australian Alps*, and other publications.

1835.—THE LITERARY NEWS.

This publication is stated to have been under the management of Mr. A'Beckett, formerly Solicitor General of the Colony. I can find no copy of it. It lasted for two or three years, and was favourably noticed by cotemporary journals.

1836.—TEGG'S MONTHLY MAGAZINE.

No. 1, March. 60 pages.

The contents are thus arranged in the first number :—(1) Introductory Address; (2) Verse, " My own Sorrows"; (3) "Fisher's Ghost," a Tale ; (4) Verse, " The Home of my Fathers"; (5) Extracts from the London *Weekly Review ;* (6) Verse, " Woman"; (7) " The Lansbys of Lansby Hall," a Tale, from *Blackwood's Magazine ;* (8) " The Boarding House," another Tale from *Blackwood ;* (9) Critical Notices of new Books ; (10) Theatrical Critiques.

Mr. Tegg was a bookseller. His magazine was neatly printed, of a small 8vo. size, and appears to have been a very readable collection of prose and verse. The former consisted almost entirely of short tales, original and selected. The conductors of these periodicals do not appear to have been particular as to the originality of their contents.

1837.—THE AUSTRALIAN TEMPERANCE MAGAZINE.

No. 1, July. Published monthly. 16 pages.

The title of this publication sufficiently indicates its purpose and general character.

1838.—THE AUSTRALIAN MAGAZINE.

No. 1, January. Published monthly. 88 pages.

The articles in the first number are very numerous and varied. They are as follows :—(1) Australia ; (2) Lines to Sir Richard Bourke, the late Governor of the Colony ; (3) " A true Story," a Tale ; (4) Poetry ; " Recollections of Naples," Canto I.

in Spenserian stanzas; (5) "Botany Bay"; (6) "Catarrh in Sheep"; (7) "Freedom of the Press"; (8) "The Dibbses," a Tale; (9) "The Administration of Sir Richard Bourke"; (10) "The Drummer," a Tale; (11) "Life of President Jackson," reprinted from the *Monthly Magazine;* (12) "General Bourke's intended Journey across the Alps"; (13) "Extracts from a Reporter's Notes—The Drunkard's Death-struggle," a Tale; (14) "The present financial situation of the Colony"; (15) "Metropolitan Ramblings," No. I.; (16) "On Human Life"; (17) "On Happiness"; (18) "The White Boys"; (19) "Zelikia, the Georgian Slave"; (20) "Everlasting Fire in Persia"; (21) Poetry, "Stars of Australia"—"The Soldier's Trust"—"Australia"; (22) Agricultural Report for December; (23) Critical notice of "The Picture of Sydney"; (24) Mathematical Questions; (25) Calendar for January.

There is certainly more variety here than is generally found in magazines; and the articles, although short, are not wanting in merit. Considering the period in which it made its appearance, it reflected credit on its conductors.

1840.—The Sydney Protestant Magazine.

No. 1, April 15. Published monthly. 32 pages.

Entirely devoted to religious matters.

1843.—The New South Wales Magazine; *or, Journal of General Politics, Literature, Science, and the Arts.*

No. 1, January. 8vo., 48 pages. With illustrations.

The early numbers of this publication are not illustrated. No. 7 contains—(1) Three well-executed engravings of public buildings in Sydney; (2) An article on "the State and Prospects of New South Wales," in which the various causes of the prevailing stagnation are stated with much force and clearness; (3)

Verse, "Oh! that I had the wings of a Dove!"; (4) "Opposite Neighbours," a Tale; (5) The Winds, their influence, &c.,—a very learned article; (6) "The last days of the Honeymoon," a Tale; (7) Review of new Works; under which title is—*first*, a favourable notice of *Tarquin the Proud, and other Poems*; *secondly*, an equally favourable notice of the comic operatic drama written by Mr. Nagel, entitled *Merry Freaks in Troublous Times*; and *thirdly*, a notice of the Prize Compositions at Sydney College; (8) Letter-press to accompany two Engravings; (9) Local Intelligence; (10) Verses, "Lines written for a Druid's Cell," and a Sonnet addressed to Charles Harpur, by Henry Parkes.

This magazine makes a very creditable appearance—quite equal, in fact, to that of any similar publication in England. Its literary merits are by no means contemptible. Taken altogether, it was a superior production to its predecessors, and indicated a fair advance in the literary capabilities of the country. Recollecting the extreme depression which existed at the time of its publication, it is surprising that such ventures should have been even thought of. In the previous year, there had been no less than seven hundred insolvencies declared—a fearful proportion to the whole population. The state of the Colony was graphically described in the November number of this magazine: "Let us then feel the pulse of the Colony, as she now lies groaning before us. What are the phenomena of the disease? The country settlers cry out that their occupation is gone; the sale of their wool, they tell us, scarcely pays the expenses of producing and sending it to market; sheep which, two or three years back, were selling at thirty shillings a head, are now gladly offered for two shillings and sixpence; merchants are breaking; high officials are defaulters; the very counsel and attorneys of the Supreme Court look grave and apprehensive of evil; our streets are almost as quiet and deserted as those of an English village; the whole community are in consternation, and men have taken to carrying their schedules about in one pocket as naturally as they do their handkerchiefs in the other." Yet, there were no less than seven newspapers and two magazines published in Sydney at this time—eight newspapers having ceased shortly before. For a population of only 30,000, this was rather creditable.

The *New South Wales Magazine* was conducted by a Mr. Slatterie, formerly of the Sydney College. It contained articles from Dr. Nicholson, now Sir Charles Nicholson; Mr. Braim, Principal of the Sydney College, and author of a *History of New South Wales*, published in 1846; Dr. Bland; Mr. (now Judge) A'Beckett, and others.

1843.—ARDEN'S SYDNEY MAGAZINE OF POLITICS AND GENERAL LITERATURE. Edited by George Arden. Illustrated by J. S. Prout.

No. 1, September. Published monthly. 8vo., 67 pages. Price, 3s. 6d.

This publication, also, is very attractive in appearance. It was commenced by a gentleman named Arden, who had been previously connected with the Press in the neighbouring Colony of Port Phillip, now called Victoria. He appears to have been under the necessity of writing the greater part of his magazine himself—a circumstance which, no doubt, hastened the final catastrophe. "Nearly the whole of the present number has been composed by the editor himself; and the exertion to produce variety in the original articles has demanded no little versatility of mood and imagination." Mr. Arden was a smart writer, and succeeded in imparting a good deal of interest to his publication. The contents of the first number are—(1) A political Essay on the "New Colonial Constitution"; (2) A satirical account of the

Aërial Machine ; (3) Biographical Memoirs, under the title of the "Representatives of the People"; (4) A humourous description of Colonial Society, under the title of "Review of the Colonial Markets"; (5) "Gilbert Christian," a Tale ; (6) The Early History of Port Phillip ; (7) Notices of British Literature ; (8) Local Intelligence of every kind ; (9) Review of Colonial Literature ; (10) Fugitive Poetry.

1844.—THE COLONIAL LITERARY JOURNAL AND WEEKLY MISCELLANY OF USEFUL INFORMATION.   16 pages, 4to. Price, 4d.

No. 1, June 27.   Published weekly.

This was not an ambitious periodical.   Some opinion of its character may be formed from the following list of articles in the 28th number :—(1) The Wheel of Time—its onward motion ; (2) Genealogy of the Queen, from *Chambers' Journal;* (3) Natural and Acquired Genius ; (4) The Conquest of Normandy, or the Monk's Three Visits, by Henry Neele; (5) Varieties ; (6) The Moralist, consisting of Moral Apothegms ; (7) Select Poetry : "Address to the New Year ;" "Old Father Time; (8) Catallactics—Article on Flax ; (9) Chemical Philosophy, on the nature of Carbon, &c. ; (10) Pearls from *Sam Slick ;* (11) Original Poetry : "Tempus Fugit "; "Lines by a Young Lady "; (12) A Tradition ; (13) English News ; (14) Advertisements.

1844.—THE PORTFOLIO OF ROMANCE, AND GAZETTE OF LITERATURE, SCIENCE, AND THE ARTS.

No. 1, July 13.   Published twice a month.

The prospectus of this publication stated that "politics would be excluded from its pages, which would be entirely devoted to—Original Tales ; Selections from the latest works of the most celebrated authors ; Poetry, original and select ; Reviews of Colonial Works ; Theatrical Notices ; Scientific Discoveries in the

Colony; Narrations of Travels in the Colony; Discoveries by Travellers; and a general Summary of News." And further, that it was "intended to blend amusement with instruction, by conveying salutary moral lessons through the pleasing and attractive medium of romance."

1848.—THE NEW SOUTH WALES SPORTING MAGAZINE. Edited by D. C. F. Scott.

No. 1, October. Published monthly. Price, 2s. 6d. 48 pages, 8vo.

This publication is remarkable for its tasteful appearance. In that respect it is superior to any similar periodical ever issued in the Colony. In addition to a handsomely illustrated title-page, it contains three neat engravings. The letter-press relates almost entirely to sporting matters: horse-racing, yachting, cricket, &c.; but at the same time, articles of a more general character are not excluded. A publication possessed of so much attractiveness had strong claims to support, but the claims do not appear to have been recognized.

1848.—THE AUSTRALIAN PENNY JOURNAL.

No. 1, Friday, 27th October. 8 pages, 8vo.

Contents of the first number:—(1) To the Public—an Editorial Statement; (2) The Golden Fleece of Australia, from Howitt's *Impressions of Australia*; (3) Education and Reform; (4) Poet's Corner: "The Native Woman's Lament," by Richard Howitt; (5) The Blue Handkerchief, a Tale; (6) Miscellaneous Extracts; (7) British Extracts; (8) Weekly Summary.

The appearance of this publication is not extremely attractive, but it was no doubt a laudable effort to distribute information among the multitude. After the 9th number it was enlarged in size, and its title altered. It then appeared as—

1849.—THE AUSTRALIAN LITERARY JOURNAL.

No. 1, Friday, 5th January. 8 pages, 4to.

Contents :—(1) Introductory Address ; (2) Ship on Fire ; (3) Original Poetry; (4) The Miser's Will, by Percy B. St. John—a Tale ; (5) Historical Parallel, relating to the French Revolution of 1830 and 1848 ; (6) A British Adventure ; (7) Miscellaneous ; (8) Almanac for 1849 ; (9) Uniform Rate of Postage : General Intelligence : Advertisements.

1850.—THE AUSTRALIAN ERA.

No. 1, August. Published monthly. Price, 6d. 16 pages, 8vo.

The *Era* appears to have been rather moderate in its literary pretensions. The contributions are stated to have been gratuitous. It makes mention of a " Professional Literary Association" as then in existence in Sydney, and the *Era* seems to have been brought out under the auspices of that Association. The 12th number concluded its existence—a fate which is editorially ascribed to the great gold discovery.

The contents of the first number are :—(1) An Essay on " Literature—its Advancement and Results"; (2) Police Reform ; (3) Stanzas, entitled " The Grave of Youth," by E.K.S. The initials are those of a gentleman named Silvester, who earned some reputation by his rhymes many years ago. He was a reporter on the *Sydney Morning Herald*, and died a few years since. His verses are gracefully executed, but they do not indicate much mental power in the author. (4) Education in New South Wales, its defects and their causes, by Edward Reeve ; (5) The Law of Copyright.

1851.—THE POLITICIAN : *a Monthly Magazine of Politics and Literature.* Conducted by Natives of the Colony.

No. 1, April. Price, 1s. 20 pages, 8vo.

The editorial address in the first number commences with the following passage :—" In forming an estimate of the character and prospects of our National Literature, one remarkable fact very strikingly presents itself to the notice of the least reflecting observer. It is—that while the Newspaper Press, with a trifling exception, is all that we can point to as evidence of our literary enterprise and ability—the barren honours to be won, even in that unproductive field, are awarded to strangers—and there is not a native of the Colony who is associated with its management in the capacity of a public writer. This is, clearly, not as it should be." The *Politician* was accordingly started to rectify this evil, but its columns were not closed to writers who did not happen to be natives of the Colony. The ability displayed in its pages is not great.

The contents of the first number are—(1) A political article, headed "The Beginning of the End"; (2) Mr. Mort and his Immigration Scheme; (3) The principles that should govern public writers; (4) On the course pursued by the Attorney General in Prosecutions for Libel; (5) Verse, "The Myall Tree." [These verses were written by Mr. Geoffrey Eagar. They also appear in No. 1 of the *University Magazine.*]

1855.—The Sydney University Magazine.

No. 1, January. Published quarterly. Price, 5s. 120 pages, 8vo.

The Sydney University was established in the year 1852. The magazine was edited and written by a few of the leading students, assisted by one or two of the Professors, especially by the late Dr. Woolley. The prospectus states:—"The proposal to establish a Sydney University Magazine has been dictated by the hope of contributing to the supply of a want already urgently felt in our community. It is time to initiate a National Literature." The existence of this periodical was limited to a very few numbers.

The first number contains—(1) A notice of Guizot's work, entitled *Shakspeare et son Temps ;* (2) An article on Railways; in which it is shewn, by the statistics of other countries, that the introduction of Railways into this Colony, which had taken place a little previously, was premature ; (3) A philosophical review of Tennyson's *In Memoriam ;* (4) Verses : " The Pearl Oyster"— " On the Death of Robert Burns"—" Suggested by the perusal of *Uncle Tom's Cabin*"; (5) Article on the Study of Law as a branch of Education, in which that study is strongly recommended ; (6) Verses : " The Sentimentalist"—" The Realist"— " The Myall Tree"—" The Bell Bird"—" Affliction"—" Recollections of Childhood"; (7) Wandering Recollections of an Optimist ; (8) A Chapter on Titles ; (9) The University and the Colleges.

This is undoubtedly the most scholarly magazine ever attempted in the Colony ; but it was deficient in the elements of popularity. It was not sufficiently light and varied to attract the ordinary run of readers.

1855.—THE AUSTRALIAN FAMILY JOURNAL : *a Weekly Magazine of Literature, Science, Arts, Mechanics, Commerce, and Domestic General Information.*

No. 1, July 3rd.   8 pages, 4to.   Price, 3d.

This publication displayed little talent of any kind. It consists mainly of extracts from English publications. Its appearance, however, is very creditable.

The first number contains the following articles—(1) " Our opening Address"; (2) " Demetrius, or the Prince of Impostors ; an historical Tale, written expressly for this magazine, by the editor"; (3) Extracts relating to "Arts, Manufactures, Mechanics, and Commerce"; (4) Under the title " Original Contribution," it is stated that "the columns for this purpose are intended for the development of native talent, of whatever style, if deserving of insertion." It does not appear, however, that "native talent" responded to the invitation, as the articles inserted are extracts. (5) "Enigmas, Charades, &c."; (6) Article on "Phrenology"; (7) Select Poetry and Prose; (8) "Science: General principles of Chemistry—Caloric"; (9) "Useful items, &c."; (10) "Our Letter Box."

1857.—THE WINDSOR REVIEW: *a Monthly Magazine of Literature, Science, and Art.*

No. 1, July. Price, 1s. 32 pages, 8vo.

The first number contains—(1) An Article on Money Orders; (2) Adele, a novelette; (3) Intelligence relating to the Windsor Debating Society; (4) Description of Windsor; (5) Gregory Pipkins, a Tale; (6) Report of the Committee of the Sydney Mechanics' School of Arts; (7) Essay on Steam Power and Railways; (8) Reviews: *Gertrude, the Emigrant*—*The Sydney Magazine of Science and Art*; (9) Verses; (10) Miscellaneous Extracts.

This periodical is distinguished rather by its usefulness than its brilliancy, but it is a creditable production for a small town in the interior.

1857.—THE AUSTRALIAN HOME COMPANION.
Published fortnightly. 28 pages.

This publication consists chiefly of miscellaneous Extracts from English publications, adapted to the comprehension of moderately intelligent readers. It appears to have merged in the

1858.—BAND OF HOPE JOURNAL, AND AUSTRALIAN HOME COMPANION.

No. 16 of which contains notice of a new religious serial, the *Australian Sunday School Monitor*, published at 1d.

1857.—The Sydney Magazine of Science and Art: containing, by authority, the proceedings of the Australian Horticultural and Agricultural Society, and the Philosophical Society of New South Wales. Edited by Mr. Joseph Dyer. Sydney.

No. 1, June. Published monthly. 20 pages, 8vo.

The first number contains—(1) A History of the "Australian Horticultural and Agricultural Society," with its Rules and By-laws, and an Address delivered by the President—Sir W. T. Denison ; (2) A History of the "Philosophical Society of New South Wales," with the Inaugural Paper of the President, Sir W. T. Denison ; (3) Remarks on Australian Wine ; (4) On the School of Arts ; (5) on Boydell's Patent Endless Railway ; (6) on Sculpture, with an account of the celebrated Mr. Woolner's stay in Sydney ; (7) Extracts from English and Foreign Scientific Journals ; (8) "Substitute for the Potato"; (9) Health of Sydney ; (10) Meteorological Report.

This publication lasted for two years, ceasing with its 24th number (June, 1859). The preface to the second volume contains some remarks, with reference to the character and fate of the magazine, which deserve attention. Alluding to the papers of the two Societies contained in the magazine, it says :—

"It is to be regretted, on public grounds, that these papers are not more widely dispersed. Previously to their appearance in this form, they were printed in the pages of the daily journals ; but in them it was found that they were buried in the more exciting topics of the day, and were rendered useless for purposes of reference, by the ephemeral character of the medium in which they appeared. In their present form they have secured the advantage of becoming permanently available. In no other form are these papers (the result of much labour and research) to be obtained. It will therefore, we trust, be acknowledged that our literary existence, should it terminate with this volume, has not been without its use.

"We never indulged the hope that a publication of this character would meet with a very large circle of readers, for scientific journals, even in England, have but a limited circulation; but we confess that we did expect that the members of the two Societies whose papers we have printed, would desire to possess the records of those bodies with which they had associated themselves. But the constant attention to business, which is characteristic of colonial life, appears very unfriendly to the development of a taste for science, literature, and art. We make no complaint concerning our want of success—perchance the encouragement that has been afforded us may be deemed by some as beyond our deserts—but we do greatly regret to see such institutions as the Agricultural and Horticultural Society, and the Philosophical Society, languishing for want of support. It is rather a reproach, too, that a wealthy community like this cannot hold out any hope of support to even one painter, poet, sculptor, or professional literary man, apart from scholastic or journalistic pursuits, and that no monthly periodical has ever yet maintained a lengthened existence in this Colony."

The magazine is excellently printed, and in every respect was well worthy of the encouragement it looked for.

1857.—THE MONTH.

No. 1, July. 56 pages. 8vo. Price, 1s.

The contents of the first number are—(1) An Essay on "Art Education in Australia"; (2) A descriptive sketch, "My Ferry Boat"; (3) "The World of Books," containing notices of recent publications in England, France, and Germany, compiled from the Reviews, &c.; (4) Review of Mr. Norton's *Australian Essays*, and other colonial publications; (5) "Life Leaves"—"The Artist at Home"; (6) Verse: "Eden Land," an unpublished ballad by the late A. J. Evelyn. [Mr. Evelyn was a man of letters, who died some few years ago in Sydney. A high opinion was formed of him by his friends, but he has left nothing in a collected shape]. "Our Australian Land"—"The Seasons, an Allegory"; (7) "On the Habits of the Water-mole," by George Bennett, Esq., a well-known Naturalist; (8) "Mr. Frank Fowler's Lecture on Coleridge"—a report; (9) "The Institutes' Chronicle"—intelligence relating to various Schools of Art. [It makes mention of a Literary Association as then existing in Sydney]; (10) Dramatic and Musical Summary—Music and the Drama at Home, from a London Correspondent; (11) Learned Societies; (12) "Wine and Walnuts," a string of jokes and witticisms; (13) "Our Letter Home," with an illustration of Mr. Mort's Dry Dock; (14) Notices to Correspondents.

This production lasted fifteen months. In many respects it is the best effort in magazine literature we have to boast of. It does not display the scholarship and general capacity of the *Sydney University Magazine*, which, in fact, approached nearer to a quarterly review than to a magazine. Its contents were of a lighter and more diversified character, and therefore more suited to the tastes of ordinary readers. Many of the articles are pungent and amusing; the notices of cotemporary European literature are written with spirit; and, altogether, the volume composed of its fifteen numbers may be read with pleasure at the present day. It was started by a gentleman named Frank Fowler, who had been connected with the London Press as a parliamentary reporter and general writer, and who had arrived in this Colony in 1855. Mr. Fowler was undoubtedly a man of considerable ability; his writings are remarkable for their liveliness and point, and he was well versed in the current literature of the day. But he belonged to what has been termed the "Cockney School" of modern writers—a school distinguished as much by its flippancy and pretentiousness as by its smartness. He came out to this Colony with the intention of creating a sensation, and he succeeded in doing so. The means adopted for this purpose was the delivery of lectures, or "orations" as he termed them. One of these consisted of a series of imitations of the chief poets of the present century, with running criticisms. It was reported at full length in the two daily papers, and the reporters were seemingly at a loss for words to express their admiration. But the imitations might have been written by any facile rhymer, and the criticisms abounded with his peculiar absurdities. He began by describing the character of the present times. They were times, he said, in which "the frescoes of Apelles were used as alehouse hatchments, and ambrosia was served up on the willow pattern." Speaking of a certain genius, he said, "His mind displayed all the convovuluted richness of a Corinthian abacus." On this passage the critical reporter exclaims, "What a world of out-of-the-way reading does that one word 'convovuluted' display! It contains the whole history of Corinthian architecture!" Carlyle's mind was compared to "an Etrurian tomb, full of old tiles and solemn rarities." So novel a style of treatment was, apparently, highly popular; but a different view of it was taken by a writer signing himself "Prometheus" (Mr. W. Forster) in the *Empire*. He pointed out its absurdities in very mild language—Mr. Fowler retorted in very angry language—the friends of either party joined the fight, and the result was an animated controversy, almost rivalling that of Dr. Newman and Mr. Kingsley. On his return to England, Mr. Fowler published a small volume entitled *Southern Lights and Shadows; being brief Notes of three years' experience of Social, Literary, and Political Life in Australia.* The book professes to give a truthful account of society in this Colony and in Victoria, with sketches of our leading men. It is in reality a ludicrous caricature of both. Here and there the book is illuminated by a sparkle of cleverness, and that, perhaps, accounts for the extraordinary fact of its having reached the dignity of a second edition. It was unworthy even of Mr. Fowler's capacity, and there is some difficulty in understanding how he came to write it.

Another contributor to this periodical was Mr. Rowe, more generally known as "Peter 'Possum," the name which he attached to his literary performances. He subsequently collected his pieces in the *Month*, and published them under the title of *Peter 'Possum's Portfolio*—a work which is mentioned in another part of this narrative. They are good specimens of magazine writing.

To what has been already said with regard to the death of the *Magazine of Science and Art*, may be added the following statements, extracted from the *Month*. The failure of so many literary journals, presenting so many claims to support, is not an easy matter to account for; and therefore, anything that tends to throw light upon it deserves attention   In the sixth number of the *Month* we are told that it had proved "a complete commercial success"; that "although each issue of the magazine costs over £130, from the very second number its returns have covered, and more than covered, its expenditure"; and that the "subscription list now numbers upwards of 2,000 names, including those of the most distinguished residents in all the Colonies." In a subsequent number, issued shortly after the one in which this jubilant statement appeared, the editor sings a very different song. After hinting at the probability of his magazine coming to a sudden stop, he proceeds to account for it. He informs his readers that, "from the time we issued our first number to the present, we have, with one or two exceptions, never received a penny from our country agents. The amount due to us from this source is over £200. We further find that no less than 900 of our own booked subscribers have never paid a shilling for the work." An article in the same magazine, on "The support of Letters in Australia," presents a very dismal picture of the literary profession in the Colony. The writer suggests, as remedies for their diseased condition, that men of wealth should employ private tutors, and asks, "Has any of our past or present Ministers engaged a private secretary?" He intimates that, unless relief is administered in some such shape, our men of genius must expect to starve.

1863.—* THE PRESBYTERIAN MAGAZINE. 30 pages, 8vo.

No. 1, January. Published monthly.

An exclusively religious periodical. It still exists.

1864.—* HORTICULTURAL MAGAZINE, AND GARDENERS' AND AMATEURS' CALENDAR ; *containing the Transactions of the Horticultural Society of Sydney.* 24 pages.

No. 1, January. Published monthly. Price, 1s.

Exclusively devoted to horticultural matters.

1865.—* THE AUSTRALIAN JOURNAL.

No. 1, 2nd September. Published weekly.

This is an imitation of the *Family Herald*, and other periodicals of the kind, which have met with so much success in London. It is printed in Melbourne, and published in Sydney and other neighbouring Colonies. Its circulation averages about 5,500 weekly, of which 1,750 are contributed by this Colony. The contents are well arranged, and are little inferior to those of its London prototype.

1865.—* THE TESTIMONY.

No. 1, October. Published monthly.

A religious publication, intended to oppose the *Presbyterian Magazine.*

POETRY.

1824.—AUSTRALASIA. By William Charles Wentworth.

This poem, as already stated, was written by Mr. Wentworth when a student at Cambridge. It did not procure the Chancellor's medal for the author. The successful poem, however, possesses no merit, either of thought or versification, which cannot be found in Mr. Wentworth's. Mr. Praed was undoubtedly a man of infinitely higher capacity as a poet than our distinguished countryman : but prize poems reduce all orders of intellect to much the same level, and, generally speaking, it is a task of some difficulty to distinguish one from another. No other effort of a poetical kind was made by Mr. Wentworth. His intellect did not tend to poetry, although it shone with so much lustre in eloquence. His College poem was published in the *Gazette* soon after it was received in the Colony, and Flanagan tells us in his History, that " great interest was aroused in regard to it, owing chiefly to the writer being a native of Australia." The last ten or twelve lines of the poem are familiar to every one in the Colony, from their perpetual quotation.

The second edition of Barrington's *Voyage to Botany Bay*, published in 1810, contains a prologue recited on the first stage erected in the Colony. Permission had been given to the convicts to amuse themselves with theatrical entertainments,—a stage was hastily constructed,—and Dr. Young's tragedy of *The Revenge* was brought out. This prologue contains two lines which are frequently quoted :—

> " True patriots we, for be it understood,
> We left our country for our country's good."

They deserve a place in Booth's collection of *Epigrams, Ancient and Modern.*

1825.—First Fruits of Australian Poetry.   By Barron
Field, Esq., F.L.S., *late Judge of the Supreme Court of New
South Wales and its Dependencies.*

Under this title, the author published a small collection of
Poems, in an Appendix to a work entitled " Geographical Memoirs
on New South Wales."   He states, in a note, that "the following
poems have hitherto been only privately printed in New South
Wales.   In consequence of the approbation which some of them
have received from several of the first poets and critics of our
times, they are now published."   In Barry Cornwall's recent
Memoir of Charles Lamb, the name of Barron Field occurs more
than once.   He is there stated to have been one of Lamb's
friends, and a member of the celebrated Thursday evening
parties.   He is also spoken of as one " well known in literature."
With such an introduction, calling up thoughts of the brilliant
contributors to the *London Magazine*, every one will turn with
some interest to Mr. Field's poetry.   How far our expectations
are gratified may be judged from the following specimen :—

BOTANY BAY FLOWERS.

" God of this planet! for that name best fits
  The purblind view which men of this ' dim spot'
  Can take of Thee, the God of suns and spheres!
  What desert forests, and what barren plains,
  Lie unexplor'd by European eye,
  In what our fathers call'd *the Great South Land !*
  Ev'n in those tracts which we have visited,
  Though thousands of thy vegetative works
  Have, by the hand of science (as 'tis call'd)
  Been murder'd and dissected, press'd and dried,
  Till all their blood and beauty are extinct ;
  And nam'd in barbarous Latin, men's surnames,
  With terminations of the Roman tongue ;
  Yet tens of thousands have escaped the search,
  The decimation, the alive-impaling,
  Nick-naming of God's creatures—'scaped it all.
  Still fewer (perhaps none) of all these flowers,
  Have been by poet sung.   Poets are few,

And botanists are many, good and cheap.
When first I landed on Australia's shore,
(I neither botanist nor poet truly,
But less a seeker after facts than truth)
A flower gladden'd me above the rest,
Shap'd trumpet-like, which from a leafy stalk
Hangs clust'ring, hyacinthine, crimson red
Melting to white.   Botanic science calls
The plant *epacris grandiflora*, gives
Its class, description, habitat, then draws
A line.   The hard of truth would moralize
The flower's beauty which caught first my eye;
But, having lived the circle of the year,
I found (and then he'd sing in Beauty's praise)
This the sole plant that never ceased to bloom.
Nor here would stop :—at length first love and fair,
And fair and sweet, and sweet and constant, pall,
(Alas for poor Humanity!) and then
The new, the pretty, and the unexpected,
Ensnare the fancy.   Thus it was with me
When first I spied the flow'ret in the grass
Which forms the subject of this humble song,
And (treason to my wedded flower) cried :—

'The Australian "fring'd violet"
Shall henceforward be my pet !'
Oh! had this flower been seen by him
Who call'd Europa's ' violets dim,
Sweeter than lids of Juno's eyes,'
He had not let this much suffice,
But had pronounc'd it (I am certain)
Of Juno's eye the ' fringed curtain'—
Pick'd phrase for eye-lid, which the poet
Has us'd elsewhere; and he will know it
Who in his drama is well vers'd :
Vide the *Tempest*, act the first.
But I am wand'ring from my duty,
First to describe my fringe-eyed beauty.
'Tis then a floss-edg'd lilac flower,
That opens only after rain,
Once, and never blows again;
Shuts, too, at early ev'ning hour,
Soon as the sun has lost its power,
Like a fairy's parasol
(If fairies walk by day at all);

Or, it may quicker gain belief,
To call it her silk neckerchief,
Dropt before she blest the place
With her last night's dancing grace ;
For surely fairies haunt a land
Where they may have the free command
Of beetles, flowers, butterflies,
Of such enchanting tints and dyes :
Not beetles black (forbidden things),
But beetles of enamell'd wings,
Or rather, coats of armour, boss'd
And studded till the ground-work's lost :
Then, for all other insects—here
Queen Mab would have no cause to fear
For her respectable approach.
Lest she should not set up her coach,
Here's a fine grub for a coach-maker,
Good as in fairy-land Long Acre ;
And very long—indeed—legg'd spinners,
To make her waggon-spokes, the sinners !
And here are winged grasshoppers ;
And, as to gnats for waggoners,
We have mosquitoes will suffice
To drive her team of atomies !
If, therefore, she and her regalia,
Have never yet been in Australia,
I recommend a voyage to us
On board the paper nautilus ;
But I incline to the opinion
That we are now in her dominion ;
Peri or fairies came from th' east,
D'Herbelot tells us so, at least ;
And we dream all those self-same dreams,
Which (from Mercutio) it seems
We owe to Mab's deliv'rancy,
As midwife and queen faëry."

In the Elia Essay on " Distant Correspondents," addressed to Barron Field, Lamb made some rather cutting jokes at our expense. None of them feels half so cutting as the " First Fruits of *Australian* Poetry," perpetrated by his esteemed correspondent.

1826.—Wild Notes from the Lyre of a Native Minstrel.
By Charles Tompson, junior. Sydney. 4to., 66 pages.

This work issued from the press of Robert Howe, and affords
a curious specimen of typography. The "Notes" consist of odes
and other lyrical pieces, displaying much smoothness of versification, but little else.

1826.—Aurora Australis: *a Specimen of Sacred Poetry for the
Colonists of Australia.* By John Dunmore Lang, D.D. and
A.M., *Presbyterian Chaplain and Minister of the Scots
Church, Sydney.* Sydney. 12mo, 165 pages.

The preface states that " the following poems, which were
written for the most part in the great South Sea, during the
author's last voyage to England, are submitted to the Australian public, in the hope of their becoming instrumental in
advancing the interests of pure religion, and promoting the
practice of virtue throughout the Colony."

The volume contains translations from the Greek and German,
and also from the Aboriginal language of the Colony. The author
did not confine his muse to strains of a pious nature. When
connected with the Press at a later period, he wrote more than
one satirical ballad, which proved his powers of ridicule and
humour. They may be found in an appendix to the last edition
of his History. Dr. Lang is a man of very versatile talent,
and could write a Hymn-book or a Comic Song-book with equal
facility.

1829.—Lays of Leisure: *a Collection of Original and Translated
Poems.* By the Rev. W. B. Clarke, A.M., *Author of the
" River Derwent," and other Poems.* London. 8vo.

A boyish production of a man of science.

1833.—AUSTRALIA : *a Moral and Descriptive Poem.* By the Author of *The Voyage.* Sydney.

The author's name was Wools. The poem, a production of moderate merit, was reviewed in the first number of the *New South Wales Magazine.*

1838.—ORIGINAL POETRY. By Beverley Suttor. Sydney. 12mo, 23 pages.

1842.—STOLEN MOMENTS : *a Short Series of Poems.* By Henry Parkes. Sydney. 8vo., 131 pages.

A collection of short lyrical pieces, originally contributed to the newspapers. The undoubted ability which the author displays as a politician does not appear in his poetry. He says in his preface, " Nearly all my poems (my book, I fear, affords another instance of the perversion of that word) have been put together in thought in 'moments' literally 'stolen' from the time occupied by the ordinary duties of a not over-happy life ; my leisure having been generally devoted to other, perhaps better, purposes." Under such circumstances, no one would look for much that was worth reading. The act of publication was justified by the author's desire to serve " the cause of Australian Literature."

1843.—TARQUIN THE PROUD, AND OTHER POEMS. Sydney. 8vo., 95 pages.

" Tarquin the Proud" is a classical tragedy, but it would not be easy to select, either from it or from the poems which accompany it, any passage that could be read with much pleasure. The author's name was S. P. Hill.

1845.—MARMONT ; *or, Suffering without Guilt: a Tale, in six Cantos.* By G. F. Poole. Sydney. 12mo., 102 pages.

The tale is simply that of an innocent man condemned and executed on suspicion of murder. It appears to have been written by an uneducated man.

1851.—MOYARRA : *an Australian Legend, in two Cantos.* Maitland. 12mo., 52 pages.

The legend tells of a blackfellow whose gin had been forcibly carried away by another blackfellow, and who, accompanied by a faithful friend, set out in pursuit of his enemy. As soon as they sighted the ravisher, the latter tomahawked the woman, and made off. He was followed to the hunting-grounds of his tribe, and attacked by the man he had injured. The latter had his revenge, but was slain by the other's friends. The author (Mr. G. W. Rusden) says in his preface, that he wrote from a feeling of gratitude to the blacks, to whom he was indebted for many acts of kindness when living in the bush. His rhymes are not without merit.

[No date.]—SHADES OF MEMORY. Sydney. 8vo., 103 pages.

The contents of this work are partly religious and partly sentimental. It was printed for private distribution, and dedicated to the author's sister.

1851.—THE AUSTRALIAN: *a Poem.* By Cato the Younger. Sydney.

1851.—RAYMOND, LORD OF MILAN: *a Tragedy of the Thirteenth Century.* By Edward Reeve, *formerly a Student of Bristol College.* Sydney. 18mo., 45 pages.

The events on which this play is founded are taken from the history of Milan, in the thirteenth century, when, under the rule of Raymond, the third Prince of the house of the Torriani. The chief event in the plot is a conspiracy, which brings about the catastrophe of the play—the murder of Mary da Romagna, and of Raymond—followed by the destruction of the assassins and the triumph of the Torriani. Mary da Romagna was, in her early years, betrothed to Raymond, but was estranged from him by his enemies. She then gave her hand to Ezzelin. Ezzelin was a claimant of the throne of Milan. He made an unsuccessful attempt to assassinate Raymond, and while under sentence of death, his life was spared at the intercession of his wife. On his liberation, Ezzelin is led to believe that his wife had succeeded with Raymond by sacrificing her honour, and is carried away by jealousy. Mary overhears the conspirators, attempts to warn Raymond, is seized and dragged before her husband. He commands her life to be taken as the forfeit of her rashness. Towards the close of the representation, many exciting incidents follow closely upon each other. The murder of Ezzelin's wife, her midnight funeral, the attack upon Raymond, and his death, the revenge accomplished immediately afterwards by a body of the Prince's troops, constitute a series of tragical events which, when properly represented, cannot fail to arrest the attention of an audience.

The author has been for many years connected with the *Sydney Morning Herald*. Apart from the difficulties which must always attend dramatic composition, so much depends upon the actor and the scene-shifter that the usual risk of failure is multiplied a hundredfold. Mr. Reeve's composition suffered greatly from the negligence with which it was put upon the stage. Intoxicated actors and giggling ballet-girls did their best to ruin it. Yet, notwithstanding these unlooked-for obstacles, the *Lord of Milan* is said to have been successful. The plot selected by the author does not admit of much variety of incident; but the composition of the play, if not marked by much dramatic genius, is at least not wanting in dignity.

1852.—Gold Pen and Pencil Sketches ; *or, The Adventures of Mr. John Slasher at the Turon Diggings.* By G. F. P., with illustrations by T. Balcombe. Sydney. 8vo., 27 pages.

A comic production. The rhymes are smooth, but deficient in taste.

1853.—The Book of the Prophet Isaiah, *rendered into English Blank Verse; with Explanatory Notes.* By John Rae, A.M. Sydney. 8vo., 270 pages.

The author proposed a difficult task to himself when he undertook to make a volume of poetry out of a literal versification of the Hebrew Prophet; but he has succeeded, so far as success can be obtained in such an effort. He justifies the work by the examples of Pope and Dryden. " I can see no reason why the bards of Israel should be less adapted for translation into English verse than those of Greece and Rome. The admirable versions of the Iliad and Æneid, by Pope and Dryden, have communicated the spirit of Homer and Virgil to thousands of English readers who never knew a word of the originals." To those who find pleasure in religious poetry, Mr. Rae's work will be very attractive ; but general readers are not likely to take much interest in a metrical rendering of the Old Testament, when the author confines himself to the words he finds in the original. Mr. Rae says, " In treating a work of so sacred a character, I have not considered myself at liberty to give wings to the *ignis fatuus* of my own fancy, and depart at pleasure from the *litera scripta* of the text." The work contains an ably written introduction, in which we have the history and character of Isaiah, and a sketch of Jewish history.

1853.—The Bushrangers, *a Play, in Five Acts; and other Poems.* By Charles Harpur. Sydney. 8vo., 126 pages.

The dramatic production with which this volume commences is not entitled to much praise, either on the score of its poetry,

H

or of the power of construction displayed in it; but at the same time, it contains passages which shew that it was written by a poet. The title of the play sufficiently indicates its character. The hero is a sentimental scoundrel, who, after receiving much kindness from a young girl, in his hours of sickness, repays her by violence, and finally murders her betrothed. Poetical justice is meted out to him at the conclusion, when he is shot down by the police; while the unfortunate heroine goes mad, and sings ditties after the fashion of Ophelia. Some comic scenes are interspersed throughout the play, in the shape of dialogues between low characters. A more unfortunate selection of a plot could hardly have been made. There is no scope for poetry, and it would be difficult for any mind, not accustomed to feed on sensation, to interest itself in the fortunes of a bush-ranger. Mr. Harpur has undoubtedly made the best of his subject; but it is much to be regretted that the labour devoted to it was not employed upon a higher theme.

Among the minor poems contained in this volume, there are one or two which evidence considerable power in the author. Chief among these is the *Creek of the Four Graves*. It is written in blank verse, and describes a tragic incident peculiar to what is termed " bush-life in Australia." A squatter had set out with four men to select a station in a part of the interior previously unoccupied by white men. They had pitched their camp for the night on the banks of a creek, and the four men had fallen asleep by the fire. Suddenly a band of savage aboriginals burst upon them, and succeed in killing those who were asleep. Their leader takes flight,—is hotly pursued,—his path is intercepted by the creek,—he plunges in, and providentially finds a large cavity in the opposite bank. Here he conceals himself, while the savages track him in vain. He then escapes to his home. All this is narrated with much dramatic force, and at each step the scene is brought vividly before the reader. The subject affords peculiar facility for the exertion of the author's powers of landscape painting—powers which constitute the chief merit of his productions. He writes like a man who has lived in the midst of those scenes of nature which he never tires in describing, and who is eminently gifted with a capacity for appreciating their beauty. A fine example of this capacity may be found in another of his poems, entitled *A Poet's Home.* Poetry of this description is obviously not suited to common apprehension, and we may thus account for the fact that Mr. Harpur's poems are not as popular as they deserve to be among his countrymen. Another obstacle to their success consists in the want of melody which characterises all his lyrical efforts, more or less. Sismondi tells us that poetry is a mixture of painting and music; Mr. Harpur gives us the painting without the music. He is extremely unmusical in every form of verse except blank verse. The latter he handles with ease—often with dignity and power. He is not always happy, moreover, in his choice of language. Whether this arises from carelessness or want of taste, is hard to say. Some of his finest passages are marred by what uneducated people call " dictionary words"— high-sounding terms compounded from the Latin, when simple Anglo-Saxonisms might have been used instead. This not only spoils the effect of his writings, but too often renders them turgid and obscure. With all these sins upon his head, however, Mr. Harpur has some true poetry in him. He has written two or three pieces which deserve to live, and will live. The greater part of his compositions will never command much admiration ; and it is unfortunate that his later efforts display no increase of power. Remembering this, it is painful to read the arrogant self-laudation in which he occasionally indulges. The idea of a man declaring himself, as Mr. Harpur does, " A Monarch of Song in the Land," is something new to Literature. If Mr. Harpur is entitled to that royal designation, he is in the unenviable position of a Monarch without subjects.

1854.—THE LUSIAD OF LUIS DE CAMOENS, *closely translated. With a portrait of the Poet ; a Compendium of his Life ; an Index to the principal passages of his Poem ; a view of the " Fountain of Tears," and marginal and annexed Notes, original and select.* By Lieut.-Col. Sir T. L. Mitchell, Knt., D.C.L. London. 8vo., 310 pages.

The translation is in the *ottava rima*, but the translator did not consider himself bound to adopt the usual rules of English versification. His stanzas are disfigured by lines of unequal syllables—varying between ten and fourteen. The effect of such a system is of course totally destructive of harmony, frequently to a ludicrous extent. The translator justifies himself on this point in the preface. " In quantity, the original varies as to the number of syllables, and in attempting an imitation in a different language, the employment of nearly as many syllables cannot, he trusts, be objected to. From ten to twelve, or even fourteen syllables, occur in one line of the original, and thus, although ten syllables is the usual quantity in *ottava rima* when imitated in English, more has (*sic*) been required in translating the lines of the *Lusiad.* By adopting a similar quantity, a tone of antiquity seems to be the result, and not unsuited, as the translator imagines, to the age of the original poem, since this is not at all affected, but the result of close imitation. It will still be found that there are fewer syllables in the translation than there are in the original."

Mickle's translation in heroic verse is objected to by Sir Thomas Mitchell, on the score of its want of fidelity to the original. Thus we have in one, poetry without fidelity, and in the other, fidelity without poetry. Sir Thomas Mitchell was an accomplished scholar, and he possessed considerable attainments in science. But his mind was not qualified to distinguish itself in poetry. " As some apology for the rough chiseling of the work," he states in his preface that it was " chiefly written under water, in a small clipper, during a voyage round Cape Horn."

Sir Thomas Mitchell was a staff officer of the Duke of Wellington, and served with distinction in the Peninsular War. He received a medal and five clasps for his gallantry in the field. He arrived in this Colony in 1828. On the death of Mr. Oxley, he was appointed Surveyor General, and in that capacity did good service to his adopted country as an explorer. His narratives of exploration will be noticed in a subsequent page. " To his skill and energy,'' says Flanagan in his History, "was due the successful construction of the principal roads by which the interior of the country was opened up for the purposes of colonization. His zeal and efficiency as Surveyor General was (*sic*) evinced in various ways, not the least of which was the execution of valuable maps and plans. He laboured successfully in the field of Science, by applying to the screw propeller the principles on which the boomerang of the New Hollander performs its wonderful gyrations in the air. To the very last he devoted himself to the discharge of his onerous duties. His death resulted from bronchitis, produced by exposure during a surveying expedition in which he had been recently engaged. He was emphatically one of those men whose career dignifies the nation among whom they live and labour."

He died in 1855.

1857.—SONGS WITHOUT MUSIC. By J. L. Michael. Sydney. 12mo., 128 pages.

[No date.]—JOHN CUMBERLAND. By J. L. Michael, Author of "Songs without Music," "Sir Archibald Yelverton," &c. Sydney. 8vo., 206 pages.

Mr. Michael has evidently a great facility in expressing his ideas poetically. His compositions are musical, and display much feeling, much liveliness of fancy, but little distinctiveness of thought. Two or three of the songs are good. " John Cumberland" is a very lengthy composition. It is a novel in verse, much in the style of Coventry Patmore's "Angel in the House." The hero is a youthful poet, who passes his time in dozing on the banks of a river. He goes to London in order to see the world, and there falls in love with a fashionable flirt. He wins her heart by an impromptu ditty, written as a trial of skill among a party of visitors. On the death of his mother, he returns to his village home, and catches a rheumatic fever. On his recovery, some months afterwards, he is surprised by not receiving any letters from the London flirt. She, it appears, had been misled by her artful mother, who did not like her engagement—went to Paris, and married a young nobleman. Meanwhile, John had made the acquaintance of two charming girls, the daughters of the country Doctor. One of them he particularly affects. Her favourable opinion was also secured by an impromptu exhibition of his poetical powers at a *conversazione;* and a fire breaking out at her house, she was rescued from destruction by her admirer. Of course they marry. All this is briskly written in a variety of measures, grave and gay. Too often, it is mere rhymed prose. Sometimes, however, the author succeeds in striking out a good thought and expressing it well. Although the poem turns almost wholly on a single hinge—that of Love—it shows little knowledge of the heart. Mr. Michael writes with too much ease, and occasionally mistakes rhyme for poetry.

1857.—THE WAVE OF LIFE : *a Poem, in three Cantos.* By D. P. Sydney. 12mo., 90 pages.

The subject of this poem, which is written in a serio-comic strain, is very simple :—A young gentleman falls desperately in love with a young lady, who jilts him, and subsequently marries an earl. The unfortunate lover becomes " a blighted being," goes to the Crimea, and disappears in battle. D. P. has undoubtedly some talent, but his book is a disappointment; he might have written better had he chosen. Good and bad lines alternate with so much regularity as to appear the result of design rather than of accident; giving his composition a tesselated sort of appearance, with alternate squares of cleverness and absurdity.

1857.—MURMURS OF THE STREAM. By Henry Parkes, late Member of the Legislative Assembly for the City of Sydney. Sydney. 8vo., 107 pages.

1858.—LYRICS: *a Collection of Songs, Ballads, and Poems.* By James Simmonds, Comedian. Sydney. 8vo., 114 pages.

The comic powers which characterised the actor do not appear to have influenced the poet, for there is no effort of a humourous character in his book. The lyrics are devoted to the expression of sentiment, and the expression is frequently good.

Mr. Simmonds is also the author of an extravaganza entitled *The Devil in Sydney,* produced in 1859.

1859.—THE MAID OF ERIN, and other Poems. By Andrew Wotherspoon. Sydney. 12mo., 126 pages.

Mr. Wotherspoon has much more patriotism than poetry in his composition. "The Maid of Erin" is a tale of '98. Miss Bertha Connor is enamoured of Mr. Rowland Dunn, a young Captain of Dragoons, stationed in Ireland. A bitter feud had existed between their families for many years; and her father, in order to keep her out of the way, sent her to a friend in Majorca. Her lover follows her in his yacht, and on his arrival, finds that Mr. Owen O'Brien, with whose father she was staying, had made unseemly proposals to her. A duel ensued, in which O'Brien is slain. Mr. Wotherspoon has very poor notions of poetry, but he tells his tale well.

1859.—SCRAPS. By Menippus. Sydney. 8vo., 116 pages.

The author of this work, which was printed for private circulation, was Mr. Robert Sealy. He was born in 1831, in Ireland, his family being of English descent, and of good extraction. He was educated at Trinity College, Dublin, but he does not appear to have remained long enough at College to take the usual degree. He then came to this Colony. On the foundation of the Sydney University, in 1852, he became a student again, and attended lectures for a term or two. He there held the reputation of a good classical scholar—a reputation which may be easily credited by any one who reads his humourous compositions. Carelessly as they were written, and little as their author may have thought of them, they are evidently the handi-work of a man quick in appreciating the beauties of language, and endowed with exquisite taste—of one, too, who had a marked faculty for reproducing the " form and pressure" of a past age, whether in old English or in Greek iambics. His career in this Colony was not a fortunate one. He was for some time a tutor in private families ; he then exchanged the drudgery of a school for the drudgery of a Government office. His death took place in 1862, when he was only thirty-one years of age.

The merit of this book might well bear a more pretentious title than its author chose to give it. Its contents are for the most part in verse. The author contented himself with such slight effusions as the mere events of the day might suggest to him ; as though he felt his only avocation was the " shooting folly as it flies." He was evidently capable, however, of much higher work than that. There are not many serious efforts among his " scraps"; but the one or two that may be found there, contain clear proof of deep feeling in their author, and of capacity to express it. As a local satirist, he was one of the most successful of our writers. The moment a bird appeared upon the wing, his fowling-piece was levelled; and he has left us many a blood-stained plume as trophies of his skill. This, perhaps, was the character in which he was most fitted to excel; but it would be an injustice to his memory to suppose (as is so often supposed in such cases) that he was not capable of higher things. The most melancholy of human beings is the low comedian; and no one, probably, is more given to pathetic feeling than he whose talent is usually exerted in creating laughter.

1862.—POEMS AND SONGS. By Henry Kendall. Sydney, 8vo., 144 pages.

This volume represents the highest point to which the poetic genius of our country has yet attained. It consists almost entirely of descriptive poems, or of poems in which the sentiment is subordinate to the description. The author paints the scenery of his native land with the hand of a master. He is superior to Mr. Harpur in this style of poetry, both in the colouring of his landscape, and in the melody of his verse. In the whole range of English descriptive poetry, there is no writer to whom Mr. Kendall can be said to bear the slightest resemblance. He is essentially original in this respect. The music to which he has set his impressions of Nature is invariably of a gloomy and despondent tone. One would think he had been "lost in the bush" at an early period of his life, and thus had learned to associate thoughts of horror with the fairest scenes. No poet in the language, from Chaucer to Tennyson, draws such dismal meanings from the external world.

Mr. Kendall's poems, however, are the production of true genius. They have not yet met with the popularity they deserve—perhaps they never will be "popular"—but there is ground to believe that the author will, in time to come, take rank among the poets of the age. It remains to be seen whether he is capable of writing in a more varied strain than he has hitherto done. Nearly all his poems are of the same character; nearly all are cast in the same mould; and this sameness, which extends to diction and metre as well as to thought and feeling, is one of the gravest objections that can be urged against them. Their author, however, is young; and greater experience, combined with a wider culture, will no doubt extend his dominion over the minds of his fellow men. The charge of obscurity is frequently urged against his compositions, and, to some extent, with justice. He, like Mr. Harpur, requires a cultivated class of readers.

The London *Athenæum* has expressed a highly favourable opinion of Mr. Kendall. After some prefatory remarks, it said:—

'Mr. Kendall has much to learn; but he has received from nature much of that strong poetic faculty and power which no amount of learning can bestow. The spirit of nearly all the writings under our hand is dark and sorrowful, but of their energy and vigour there can be little doubt. [Two of Mr. Kendall's poems are here extracted—"The River and the Hill" and "Kiama."] The peculiar mark of Kendall's genius—a wild, dark, Müller-like power of landscape-painting—is less visible in these pieces than in the following one [The poem "Fainting by the Way" is extracted.] Most readers who examine the structure of these compositions will agree with us that a man who can execute such work at the age of twenty, may hope, in his riper years and experience, to be heard of again in the world of letters."

The same journal, in its issue of the 17th February, 1866, contained the following article on Mr. Kendall:—

"Mr. Kendall, who has before sent us poems from which we have given extracts in our columns, and who now sends us a bulky MS., accompanied by a very sensible letter, has really legitimate claims to attention. 'In my spare hours,' he says, 'and whenever health and the choking troubles of a really hard life have suffered me, I have written and written on; and the accompanying verses, alive, as they must be, with a certain intensity of feeling, and naturally shadowed with a remarkable gloom, are at least the genuine results, or some of them.' He adds, that he is very anxious for the existence and recognition of an indigenous native Literature, and suggests that we should devote an article to the subject. This we should be prepared to do, were the materials at our command sufficient for the purpose; but with only Mr. Moore's volume, Mr. Kendall's manuscript, and a few poor extracts from the poems of Mr. Charles Harpur, we can form no clear idea of what Australian poetry is, or is likely to become. Concerning Mr. Kendall's personal work, however, we can speak hopefully. The manuscript he has sent us contains, among much that is poor and imitative, a certain portion that is very good indeed—so good, that we believe a careful study of indigenous subjects may lift the writer to a very high place among colonial poets. 'Elijah' and 'Rizpah'—two allegorical poems about America—are such as anybody might have written, and as few people would find it worth their trouble to write; possessing only one noticeable feature—the carefully chosen use of scriptural phrases. None of the meditative pieces rise above common-place; but the two poems on indigenous subjects are full of strength and vigour. Nothing, indeed, could be better than this song. [The "Song of the Cattle Hunters" is here quoted.]

"Excellent in another way is 'Ghost Glen,' a poem which, once read, must linger on the memory in its weird horror. [The poem is here quoted, and the article concludes with the following:]

"If Mr. Kendall continues to exert his faculty as successfully as he has done in these two pieces, England as well as Australia will gladly recognise his place as a singer. He has both disadvantages and advantages in his distant sphere, but the latter preponderate. He occupies virgin soil—stands in the midst of a society whose characteristics have never yet been mirrored in song; while English writers are throwing up their pens yearly, because they can assimilate nothing new. Let him seek in the great life around him those human forms of humour, pathos, and beauty, which, touched by the gifted hand, cannot fail to win the hearts of the public; and let him use his local colouring—a precious treasure—to illustrate truths which are universal. It is impossible, of course, to say how he would succeed in the profounder labour of dramatic insight—such faculty as he shews in the poems before us being distinctively a lyrical faculty; but that he has gifts there can be no question; and his communication to us is so modest and sensible, that we are assured he will put those gifts to the best use, leave his imitative efforts behind, and strike out in the path which he is most suited to explore."

Mr. Kendall was born in 1842, and is a native of the Colony.

1864.—Spring-life Lyrics.   By J. S. Moore.   Sydney.   8vo.,
180 pages.

The author has been an industrious contributor to the
journalism of the Colony for many years past.   He candidly
avows in his preface that he is " no poet," and the confession has
been endorsed by the *Athenæum*.   " Mr. Moore confesses that he
is no poet, and, as we quite agree with him, it would be useless to
criticise or quote his effusions."   It would not be too much to
say, however, that Mr. Moore can write a very fair song for the
pianoforte.

1865.—Poems.   By J. L. Brereton, M.D., Author of " The
Travels of Prince Legion" and other Poems.   London.   8vo.,
159 pages.

The chief feature in these poems is the strongly-marked
vein of religious feeling running through them, and which must
recommend them to those readers who seek the religious element
in literature.   They are all neatly executed.   The Colony is
indebted to Dr. Brereton for the introduction of the Turkish
Bath.

1865.—The Tower of the Dream.   By Charles Harpur.   Reprinted from *The Australian Journal*.   Sydney and Melbourne.
8vo., 24 pages.

This work is not by any means calculated to increase the
number of Mr. Harpur's admirers.   As the latest production of
a man who has spent a lifetime in writing poetry, it is to be
regretted that his efforts have not resulted in something better.

Perhaps there is no gentleman in the Colony who has written
a larger quantity of verse than Mr. Henry Halloran.   For the
last thirty or forty years, he has been in the habit of contributing
poetical compositions to the various newspapers and literary

periodicals of the time. He is, in fact, the Poet Laureate of the Colony. Few events of more than ordinary interest have been suffered to pass into oblivion without some commemorating lines from his prolific pen. From the ease with which he casts his thoughts and feelings into poetic shape, his verse too often assumes the appearance of doggrel.

There are other pieces from his pen, however, of a much loftier vein, and in these he has displayed an unbounded love of nature, deep sympathy with the highest aspirations of the soul, and infinite sensibility. Too often he loses himself in a mist of obscurity—a common failing with our poets, apparently arising from a belief that poetry has nothing to do with the common sense and common apprehension of mankind. Some of his minor efforts are pleasing, but there is nothing from his pen that seems to have met with very general favour. It is to be regretted that no collection of his fugitive pieces has yet appeared.

FICTION.

1841.—A LOVE STORY. By a Bushman. Sydney. 2 vols., 8vo.

There are three or four love stories in this work instead of one, and none of them involves any complexity of incident. The author does not seem to have troubled himself much about a plot. He introduces his reader into an aristocratic family, and then takes him to Malta, where a young gentleman in the Army— a connection of the aristocratic family—has got himself into a difficulty, by falling in love with a Greek girl, and nearly killing his friend in a duel. His brother arrives to get him out of it, and discovers that his reason is affected. The doctor advises that a marriage should take place between the Greek girl and her infatuated lover. The ceremony is performed, and the party start for Italy. Here the work becomes quite a guide-book; the author displaying, with evident satisfaction, his familiarity with the leading features of continental travel. On their way to Rome, the Greek catches the marsh fever, and dies; her lover again loses his reason, and after some adventures on the way, dies suddenly. The disconsolate brother pursues his travels, and ultimately returns to England. There he makes preparation for his marriage with a certain Julia to whom he had been attached before his departure. Everything is arranged, the bridegroom goes to London for a few days, and on his return, is horrified to find a funeral *cortége* drawn up at the door of the mansion where he expected to meet his Julia. She too had died during his absence; and he sets out again on his travels, finally turning up in Australia.

There is an immense amount of sentiment worked up in this love story, and the writing is executed in the rhapsodical style so popular in fashionable novels forty or fifty years ago. The "Bushman" breaks out into fervent moralizing at every step, and is quite uncontrollable when the theme turns upon the mysteries of love. Thus he exclaims: " Woman! dearest woman!

born to alleviate our sorrow and soothe our anguish! who·canst bid feeling's tear trickle down the obdurate cheek, or mould the iron heart till it be pliable as a child's. Why stain thy gentle dominion by inconstancy? Why dismiss the first form that haunted thy maiden pillow until—or that vision is a dear reality beside thee—or thou liest pale and hushed on thy last couch of repose?"

The work is dedicated to Lady Gipps; and in the title-page of a copy in the collection of the late Mr. Justice Wise, is stated to have been written by Major Christie, late Postmaster General of the Colony.

1852.—TALES FOR THE BUSH. By Mrs. Frances Vidal. Originally published in Australia. Fourth edition, enlarged. London. 12mo., 386 pages.

These tales, which have a moral and religious tendency, were first published in Sydney, in numbers.

1857.—GERTRUDE, THE EMIGRANT; *a Tale of Colonial Life*. By an Australian Lady. With numerous Engravings. Sydney. 8vo., 193 pages,

The authorship of this work is attributed to Miss Atkinson, of Windsor. It is a production of more than average merit, and displays a considerable talent for novel-writing. The scene is laid wholly in this Colony, principally in the bush; and nowhere are the peculiar features of bush life more accurately or more graphically pourtrayed. The tale abounds in incident, the characters are skilfully drawn, and the literary execution is quite equal to that of ordinary novels. The authoress is too fond, perhaps, of obtruding moral and religious reflections upon her reader, being evidently a member of that mistaken class which looks upon fiction as an appropriate channel for the conveyance of religious edification. Her descriptions of Australian scenery are extremely good: anyone who has resided in the bush will recognize the faithfulness of her landscapes. The best character in the book is that of the "new chum"—a supercilious coxcomb, who goes up-country with the idea of ridiculing the natives, and is signally discomfited. The contrast between this gentleman and the old residents in the bush, including the good old convict lady, the country doctor, and the young superintendent, is brought out remarkably well. Then there are several detached scenes which fix themselves in the memory ; such as the child struck by a falling bough while playing at the foot of a "woolly gum-tree"; the "Dead Man's Run," where the skeleton of a lost wanderer in the bush is discovered by a party of young stockmen ; the narrow escape from a mob of wild cattle, careering down the side of a precipitous hill ; and other incidents presented by bush life. The result of the whole is a strong impression that the authoress did not mistake her vocation in attempting to write a novel, and that the cultivation of her faculty for fiction would certainly lead to success.

"Gertrude" originally appeared in numbers. The illustrations are bad.

1859.—COWANDA, THE VETERAN'S GRANT ; *an Australian Story*. By the Authoress of "Gertrude," &c., &c. Sydney. 8vo., 135 pages.

A simple story, the details of which are not exciting, either in themselves or in the manner in which they are related. They consist principally of the adventures of a young man, of good disposition but weak principle, who runs away from a merchant's office to the "Diggings," to the great grief of his relatives. By an artful contrivance on the part of a rascal who had some acquaintance with his family, he is suspected of having forged his grandfather's signature to a cheque, and his sudden retreat from business is accounted for on the supposition of his guilt. He is ultimately restored to his friends ; and we are informed, in the last chapter of the book, that the real forger was drowned at sea, on his way to California, by the foundering of his ship. The authoress loses no opportunity of enforcing the claims of religion upon the attention of her reader.

This work is in no respect equal to its predecessor, and consequently is a disappointment. It contains no character, good or bad, to which we feel ourselves attracted, and altogether there is a "small tea-party" atmosphere about it that few readers can be supposed to relish. The authoress has made no other literary effort since the publication of this tale, beyond contributing a few articles on the botany of the country to a daily journal. This is much to be regretted.

1859.—BOTANY BAY. By John Lang, Esq., Barrister-at-Law. Author of "Too Clever by Half," "Wanderings in India," "The Forger's Wife," &c. London. 8vo. 238 pages.

The author makes the following communication in his preface :—" To my readers in Australia—the land of my birth—I desire to say that I do not hold myself responsible for the sentiments of the various persons whom I have introduced as ' characters'; and that when I have spoken of the Colony as ' Botany Bay,' it was not my intention to be either sarcastic or insulting. An absence of nearly twenty years from the Colony— partly in India, and partly in Europe—has in no way lessened my regard for the land where the days of my boyhood were spent, and where I yet hope to end my life ; and I would here desire to express, that it afforded me great joy to find that the prophecy in which I indulged at the public meeting at the Sydney College, in 1842, when I inconsistently seconded Mr. W. C. Wentworth's resolution, that the Crown be petitioned to grant the Colony a Representative Assembly, was not fulfilled, but falsified. I was then a very young, and perhaps a silly and selfish man, when I propounded in public that the Colony was not ripe for any Government save that of a purely Crown Government ; and the severe handling I received from the entire Press of the Colony was no doubt well merited ; for assuredly I was not justified in agreeing to second so important

I

a resolution, and then express such strong doubts as to the advisability of its being carried into effect. The unpopularity that I incurred during the few months that I remained in the Colony after my speech at the Sydney College, was, I trust, regarded as a sufficient punishment for that 'youthful indiscretion' on my part."

Mr. Lang's reputation as a popular writer is well known to every reader of fiction. "Botany Bay" is by no means the least graphic and amusing of his works. The various legends of the Colony which he has treated in the form of fiction are familiar to every old resident among us, while the embellishments with which he has surrounded them render them doubly interesting. Few works of the kind are better worth reading.

1866.—FIFTY YEARS AGO : By Charles De Boos, Author of the "John Smith Letters," the "Poor Man," "Random Notes," &c. &c. Sydney.

"Fifty Years Ago" is a serial tale, now in course of publication in fortnightly parts. The object of the author is to illustrate the state of society in this Colony in the days of its infancy, when the interior was scarcely known to white men, and the aboriginals had not yet been ruined by contact with civilisation. The first part describes a cruel massacre perpetrated by three blacks upon the wife and children of a settler, during his absence ; the crime being committed for the purpose of obtaining his small possessions. The second describes the pursuit and capture of the murderers by the settler and his son. The latter have made a strange vow to shoot one of the savages on each anniversary of the crime, and to place one of his hands on the grave of their relatives. After the blacks are informed of this project, they are set at liberty. The third part introduces the reader to the society of a miller and his daughter, and to two men living on the farm, one of whom is an accepted sweetheart, and the other a jealous rival. The work is well written, and promises to make a very good novel. Its delineation of old times is exceedingly life-like, while there is no lack of incident to fix the attention of the reader.

Mr. De Boos is a reporter to the *Herald*, and has at various times contributed sketchy articles to its columns. Four years ago there appeared in that journal a series of letters, signed " John Smith, of Congewoi," in which the political characters of the day were photographed with much sarcastic humour. The letters displayed a very accurate knowledge of bush life, and the style in which they were written was peculiarly racy and original. They are now being re-published in a separate form.

1867.—Australian Capers: *or, Christopher Cockle's Colonial Experience.* By " Old Boomerang." London, 8vo.

This work is advertised to appear in February next. The author (Mr. J. R. Houlding) informs us in a prospectus, that " the main object of the above work is to warn parents in England and elsewhere from sending their inexperienced sons to Australia with large capital, and their young daughters without protection." Under the name of " Old Boomerang," Mr. Houlding has contributed amusing sketches to the *Sydney Mail* for many years past.

* * * *

A young writer, Mr. F. S. Wilson, has contributed several tales to our periodical literature—" Woonoona," " Shot through the Heart," " Broken Clouds," &c. They are not devoid of merit, and it is quite possible that their author may hereafter achieve distinction as a novelist. He has also written a good deal of verse. The style seems to be rather a reflection of Kendall's, but Mr. Wilson is not wanting in force of conception, harmony, and feeling. A collection of his various efforts might be read with pleasure.

ORATORY.

1853.—THE SPEECHES IN THE LEGISLATIVE COUNCIL OF NEW SOUTH WALES, *on the Second Reading of the Bill for forming a new Constitution for the Colony.* Edited by E. K. Silvester. Sydney. 228 pages, 8vo.

The debate referred to in the title was the most important, and certainly the most dignified, that ever took place in the Legislature of the Colony. The passing of the Constitution Act altered the whole political system of the country, and largely affected its social system also. That the importance of the occasion was fully felt by the Members of the Council is evident from their speeches, all of which exhibit proof of the most careful elaboration. The community had been agitated for many years previously on the subject of legislative reform; and the debate of 1853 represented the last of their great constitutional struggles.

The collection edited by Mr. Silvester contains some highly creditable displays of rhetorical and argumentative power—displays, in fact, that would do honour to any deliberative assembly in Europe. The most remarkable speeches were those delivered by Mr. Wentworth, who moved the second reading—by Mr. Martin, who strenuously supported the measure—and by Mr. Darvall, who as strenuously opposed it. The last-named gentleman was one of the ablest men, and certainly one of the most accomplished advocates, that ever adorned the Colony. In the speeches of these gentlemen, the antagonistic principles of Conservatism and Democracy were finely contrasted. The first, who was in fact the author of the Bill, spoke of it as one "framed with the express object of arresting the inflow of democracy"; and a great portion of his speech was occupied with a comparison between English and American institutions, much to the disadvantage of the latter. The second followed with a similar line of argument. The third, who could by no means be justly spoken of as a democrat, yet occupied the position of "leader of the democratic party." He advocated the infusion of a larger share of the popular element in the proposed Constitution; and at the same time defended the American form of government from the disparaging remarks of Mr. Wentworth. Each of these gentlemen spoke with much eloquence, and each supported his arguments by abundant quotations from eminent writers.

Mr. Wentworth's career in public life was of long duration. It extended over a period of thirty years, from 1824, when he returned to the Colony, to 1854, when he quitted it. One of the first practising barristers, he retained the lead of that profession as long as he continued in practice. Although he had more than one able competitor, he may be said to have remained, from first to last, without a rival. Several members of the Bar, in days gone by, were men of far more than ordinary capacity; as, for instance, Dr. Wardell, Mr. Robert Lowe, and Mr. Richard Windeyer. But there was none who possessed the massive intellectual power, combined with the overpowering declamation, of Mr. Wentworth. These qualifications marked him out as the Pericles of our small State; and whether at the Bar or in the Council, he was universally regarded as the foremost man in the country. His eloquence was not distinguished by any marked display of imaginative power, nor by the studied grace of language. It was remarkable rather for its declamation, for its fiery scorn of his opponents, for its irresistible flow of logical sentences. Whatever the matter that called him to his feet, he · dealt with it in such a style as showed a masterly grasp and comprehension of his subject. There were few weak points in his intellectual armour. The characteristic of his intellect was strength—not strength devoid of beauty, but strength in a greater degree than beauty. Compared with Mr. Robert Lowe's, his oratory differed from that distinguished speaker's in much the same manner that a statue of Hercules would differ from a statue of Apollo. In the one, our attention would be attracted by the prodigious development of muscle—in the other, by the exquisite grace and finish of its outline. His speech on the Constitution Bill was not the highest effort of his eloquence, but it furnishes a fair specimen of his powers. In no part of it does he display much splendour of imagery or much gorgeousness of diction—these were qualities of oratory which he rarely affected; but he maintains throughout a solid line of argument, and a lofty tone of declamation, admirably suited to the circumstances under which it was delivered. The historian Flanagan pronounces it one that "fully confirmed his reputation as one of the first of living orators." The phrase may seem exaggerated; and it is not probable that Mr. Wentworth's name will descend to posterity with those of Gladstone, D'Israeli, and Bright. His fame must be confined to the land which gave him birth—and in that land it rests on a basis that will last for ever.

Mr. Martin has been, for some years past, the most distinguished Member both of the Legislature and the Bar. He took an active interest in politics at an early period of his career; and although he has had much opposition to encounter, his reputation for ability has steadily increased. Many of his speeches have been deservedly admired; but the qualities displayed in them are rather those of a fluent, compact, and powerful speaker than of a great orator. Clearness of statement, conciseness of expression, force of argument, and ample mastery of his subject, characterize all his public utterances.

Intellectual power of a very high and very peculiar order was displayed by Mr. Darvall. Acute, sarcastic, logical, skilled in all the technicalities of the Courts, and in all the solemnities of Parliament, he possessed a coolness, a self-command, a presence of mind, that seemed almost incompatible with ordinary blood and nerves. He would have been a marked man in the most brilliant circle of politicians or lawyers that ever met in England.

Not that he was a brilliant man himself—there was nothing brilliant about him ; but he presented a singular combination of coolness and power which could not fail to fix attention and command respect. In addressing a public audience, his delivery was characterized by extreme ease. Language presented no difficulties to him. A well balanced flow of sentences he had always at command. But the language he chose never displayed the fancy-work of an artist—it was merely the common-place material best fitted to express his thoughts.

Mr. Darvall left the Colony in 1865, after a very lengthened residence, and a very prominent career. He was four times Attorney General.

Mr. Robert Lowe—now one of the most eminent Members of the House of Commons—resided in this Colony from 1842 to 1850. During that period he was for several years a Member of the Legislative Council, and he was also engaged in practice at the Bar. It is needless to speak of the character of his eloquence. He displayed considerable interest in the politics of the time, and the reports of many a brilliant speech may still be read in our journals.

Mr. Deniehy's capacity as a public speaker has already been noticed. Previous to his election as a Member of Parliament, he delivered more than one speech which deservedly gained the highest approbation. On the occasion of a great public meeting, held to protest against certain features in the Constitution Bill, he made a speech which has frequently been referred to since, as one of the finest oratorical efforts ever listened to in the Colony. His eloquence was perhaps of a higher order than that of others who have gained a wider reputation. It was the eloquence of a brilliant man of letters, contrasted with the eloquence of a politician—of one endowed with rare power of imagination, and a skill in the use of words found only in the great masters of style.

As a public speaker, there are few who can better stand the test of criticism than Mr. Dalley. To a perfect command of language, and intuitive good taste in its selection, he adds an irresistible force of humour, and a happy facility in ridicule which often outweighs the most elaborate logic. His speeches seldom bear any marks of elaboration; the "midnight oil" business has no attractions for him; but his efforts—if efforts they can be called—are none the worse for being unpremeditated. He exercises a powerful influence over the feelings of his audience, and in that respect he is not excelled by any gentleman we have named. Eloquence is rarely heard in Courts of Law, but Mr. Dalley's speeches at the Bar are entitled to rank among the most brilliant displays of forensic oratory, either in this or in any other country.

1863.—THE RIVERINE QUESTION. *Speeches in the Legislative Assembly of New South Wales.* Melbourne. 240 pages, 8vo.

There is little or nothing that can be called eloquent in this collection, the subject being of too practical a nature to admit of it. The speeches were collected and published by the squatting party, as a record of opinion on a question in which they were greatly interested.

1863.—THE NEW SPEAKER, *with an Essay on Elocution.* By John Connery. Sydney, 8vo.

A similar compilation to Knowles's "Elocution." The selection of extracts shews considerable taste, and the original writing prefixed to them is excellent. The author is a Clerk in the Legislative Assembly.

HISTORY.

1819.—A Statistical, Historical, and Political Description of the Colony of New South Wales and its dependent Settlements in Van Diemen's Land : *with a particular enumeration of the advantages which these Colonies offer for emigration, and their superiority in many respects over those possessed by the United States of America.* By W. C. Wentworth, Esq., a Native of the Colony. London. 465 pages, 8vo.

Three editions of this work were published in the course of five years. The second, enlarged to 579 pages, appeared in 1820, and the third in 1824, as a work in two volumes. It performed a service of very great value to the Colony ; in the first place, by exposing the evils to which the Colony was subjected under the arbitrary form of government established in it ; and, in the second place, by pointing out the various advantages it offered as a field for emigration. The author was evidently actuated by highly patriotic views. " His only aim," he stated in his preface, " in obtruding this hasty production on the public, is to promote the welfare and prosperity of the country which gave him birth ; and he has judged that he could in no way so effectually contribute his mite towards the accomplishment of this end, as by attempting to divert from the United States of America to its shores, some part of that vast tide of emigration which is at present flowing thither from all parts of Europe." It is not clear that the publication of the work succeeded in this particular object ; but there is no doubt that it attracted a great deal of attention, and caused the removal of many obstacles from the path of colonial prosperity. The first edition formed the basis of an article in the *Edinburgh Review*, in which the subjects of complaint dwelt upon by Mr. Wentworth were alluded to, and the justice of his remonstrances avowed. In the course of two or three years afterwards, the Home Government modified the administration of the Colony, by the establishment of a Legislative Council. This was the first step in the progress from an arbitrary to a representative form of government ; and it is fair to conclude that the action of the Colonial Secretary at home was hastened by the powerful logic of Mr. Wentworth.

It is frequently said that good speakers make bad writers. Mr. Wentworth was pre-eminently a speaker ; and if there be anything in this adage beyond its epigrammatic expression, it might be expected that his writings would possess no merit. This is not the case. The literary execution of his History betrays no inexpertness with the pen. It is spoken of in the preface as " a hasty production, originating in the casual suggestion of an acquaintance." There is evidence of this assertion in some portions of it. The first part of the work is occupied with topographical remarks, and was evidently written for the benefit of emigrants. Here the author certainly does not rise beyond the average of " Guides to Emigrants." But the chapter on the " influence of the existing system of government" is full of vigorous writing, and some passages might be quoted for their eloquence. Where the author touched upon political matters, he was evidently breathing a congenial atmosphere—his lungs expanded and his cheeks glowed. The third edition of his work gave him an opportunity of replying to the celebrated Report of Mr. Commissioner Bigge—a gentleman who had been sent out to inquire into the state of the Colony. This report was extremely damaging to the Governor, Lachlan Macquarie ; and it strongly condemned the system on which the Governor had acted—that of patronizing reformed convicts. On this subject, as already stated, the Colony was split up into two factions. Of one of these factions, which regarded Governor Macquarie with feelings of the warmest admiration, Mr. Wentworth was by far the most able and the most eloquent supporter. The indignation created in this section of society by Mr. Bigge's report may be easily imagined by any one who will take the trouble to read it ; but that indignation must have been greatly soothed—if its tones were not converted into the tones of triumph—when they read the bitter exposure of " the booby Commissioner," the animated defence of Macquarie, and the just and manly vindication of the Emancipist cause, written by their talented leader.

Although this work is generally termed a History, there is little in it that is strictly historical. What there is, is merely incidental. The author had no intention to write a professed History. He addressed himself to emigrants on the one hand, and to politicians on the other.

1824.—An Historical Account of the Colony of New South Wales and its dependent Settlements, *in illustration of Twelve Views, engraved by W. Preston, a Convict, from Drawings taken on the spot by Captain Wallis, of the 46th Regiment. To which is subjoined an accurate Map of Port Macquarie, and of the newly discovered River Hastings.* By J. Oxley, Esq., Surveyor General of the Territory. Folio.

The only trace of this work that I can find is in the *Gentleman's Magazine* for 1824, which contains a short article on New South Wales, quoting Mr. Oxley's work and the third edition of Mr. Wentworth's History. Respecting the former, it adds :—" The engravings in this volume are curious and interesting, as being the first specimen of the graphic art which this infant community has produced. They are engraved on the common sheet copper used for ships, it being impossible to procure a single copper-plate fit to engrave upon in the Colony."

Mr. Oxley died in 1828, having held the office of Surveyor General for sixteen years. His services to the Colony, especially in the dangerous task of exploration, were considerable. He has left behind him a lasting memorial—the Journal of his Expedition into the Interior.

1834.—AN HISTORICAL AND STATISTICAL ACCOUNT OF NEW SOUTH WALES, *both as a Penal Settlement and as a British Colony*. By J. D. Lang, D.D. London. 2 vols., 8vo.

A second edition of this work was published in 1837, and a third, considerably enlarged, in 1852. It is more entitled to the name of History than Mr. Wentworth's book; but if the reverend author designed his work upon what he conceived to be the ordinary principles of historical architecture, his notions of those principles must have been rather vague. A large number of its pages are occupied with details which would have been highly appropriate in an autobiography. A casual glance at the " contents" will show how much " the Author" figures in the work. There are few chapters in which the reader is not entertained with an account of " the Author's" doings and sufferings, or in a *réchauffé* of " the Author's" squibs and leading articles. This is a lamentable weakness in a man of great ability. It vitiates an excellent work. If the author's purpose in its composition was to gain a triumph over his adversaries, he may have succeeded in doing so; but that success involved the forfeiture of the reputation which might otherwise have been gained as an impartial historian.

Although Dr. Lang is an indefatigable writer, he never seems to have paid much attention either to his matter or his manner. There is little evidence of revision in his pages, although there is much of the necessity for it. Possessed of a ready pen, he appears to have set down his thoughts in the first terms that occurred to him, and to have troubled himself no more about them. This is to be regretted ; for the rough-hewn blocks of his intellectual masonry shew how grand a structure they might have served to form. Nature had qualified him to shine in more than one great field of intellectual energy. Equally philosophical and practical—fertile in theory, and sound in argument—with a great capacity for research, and a lively sense of humour—he might have left behind him more than one monument of rare intellectual powers. All his works are valuable, but all are slovenly in their execution. They have been hastily put together in thought, and hastily thrown into shape by the pen. They have been rather the occupation of his leisure hours, than the object of his unremitting industry. Works indeed which might have absorbed the intellectual energies of smaller men, have been to him merely the pastime of his holidays.

He speaks candidly in his preface of these objections to his workmanship, and explains the circumstances which have given rise to them :—" Having, unfortunately, had to spend a large portion of his life at sea, the author has latterly found it expedient and necessary, independently altogether of other and higher objects, to carve out beforehand sufficient literary labour for each successive voyage, to redeem that portion of his life from the mere blank which it might otherwise present, as well as to escape the listlessness and languor into which any person without an absorbing employment is, in such circumstances, likely to fall. The historical portion of the work was written in the South Pacific, and the statistical in the Atlantic ; the month occupied in both oceans in the Cape Horn part of the voyage having been spent in the composition of another work, which is now issuing from the press, simultaneously with these volumes."

No account of this Colony has met with more notice from the English Press than Dr. Lang's, and probably none has been more largely circulated. It cannot be doubted that the various editions of his History have done more to affect public opinion at home, with regard to this country, than any other publication. It is a matter of some interest to observe the tone of English criticism on these matters ; and, as the character of the reverend author has been bitterly attacked, it is also interesting to hear the judgment of impartial tribunals. For these reasons, the following extracts will deserve perusal.

One of the first reviews of the History was written by the late G. L. Craik, Professor of English Literature in Belfast College. It appeared in a periodical called the *Printing Machine*. Towards the end of his remarks, Mr. Craik said :—

"The latter part of the work is devoted to the state of morals and religion in New South Wales ; and this subject leads the author to the history of his own exertions in founding the most important institution for education which the Colony contains—the Australian College. Even upon certain speculative points which present themselves prominently in the course of his expositions, Dr. Lang's convictions have evidently all the strength of passion. Declaring frankly, and at once, that we cannot sympathize with him, either in his vehement preference of Scotland and Scotchmen to every other land and people under heaven, or in his violent anti-episcopalianism, we bear our willing testimony to the high-mindedness he evinces in the whole tone and tenor of his remarks, even when, as we conceive, his feelings are most prejudiced and misdirected. We certainly think that his scorn for those who differ from him as to certain matters sometimes more than approaches the verge of intolerance ; but, on the other hand, we acknowledge that he has had great provocation to feel as he does. To his book itself we must refer our readers, for a full detail of his arduous, persevering, and noble struggles for the great object on which he had set his heart—the establishment of the first seminary for dispensing education in the higher branches of literature and science throughout his adopted country. We do not say that every step he took in his efforts to forward this object was the most prudent or judicious in the world. We think that, without any sacrifice of principle, he might have conciliated more of those adverse interests which he attempted either to set at defiance, or at least to stand independent of ; and we are also of opinion that, if he had pursued his object in a somewhat less pre-eminently Scottish and Presbyterian spirit, not only would he have met with much less opposition, but he would have done much more good. The manner, however, in which his disinterested exertions were thwarted, from too many quarters, and from some quarters whence he might most have counted upon encouragement and assistance, can only be characterized as paltry and discreditable in the extreme. The miserable jealousy which he encountered on the one hand, the direct attempts which were made to crush and destroy him on the other, and the coldness and desertion which, as soon as the efforts of power were thus directed against him, he experienced from many of those who had at first professed to stand his friends, exhibits all the worst and meanest vices of provincial society."

The first edition of his History was also reviewed in the *New Monthly Magazine*, as follows :—

" The Colony of New South Wales has, of late years, excited unusual interest, in consequence of the tide of emigration having, in a great measure, set in that direction. The extent of our information, however, respecting the real condition and resources of the Colony has been hitherto very limited ; and thousands of those who quitted this country to settle there, could, at best, be only said to be taking a leap in the dark. This need no longer be the case ; if it be, emigrants will have themselves to blame, for in the volumes before us we have a most ample and minute account of New South Wales. We have never, indeed, seen a more complete or valuable work of the kind. We cannot conceive of anything further that Dr. Lang has left us to desire. The person who reads his work with attention may form almost as good an idea of the climate, the soil, the capabilities of the country, and of its moral, its social, and political condition, as if he had spent a " seven years' " residence in it. We had previously read a good deal respecting New South Wales, yet our information on the subject was not only limited, but incorrect. In fact, until the appearance of Dr. Lang's volumes, there was no work on the subject which was worth perusing. The only blemish we can discover in the work is, that the author is sometimes unduly severe when speaking of men of whose conduct he disapproves. We could have wished that he had contented himself with simply condemning the improper actions, and not giving his invectives the appearance of personality. We wish it to be understood, however, that we concur with the author, in almost every instance, in the condemnatory opinions he expresses: we only differ with him in some

iustances as to the manner in which his disapprobation is expressed. The
work, we repeat, is one of great value. It is replete with the most interesting
information, and cannot fail to become a standard work for many years to
come.''

On the publication of the third edition, the following criticism appeared in the *Westminster Review* :—

" Dr. Lang's *Historical and Statistical Description of New South Wales*,
now in its third edition, is so much improved and enlarged as to merit the
consideration due to a new work. No man has written so fully and intelli-
gently about Australia as Dr. Lang. His *Cooksland*, his *Phillipsland*, and
the present work combined, contain a vast amount of information, which
only a thirty years' residence in the country, and a warm interest in its
welfare, could have collected ; for it is chiefly the result of personal observation made during extensive tours in every direction. His life has been a very
stirring one, according to his own account of it ; and he *does* give an account
of it—so minute, indeed, that he might have entitled his work, *The History
of Dr. Lang, to which is added, the History of New South Wales*. The
Doctor is an amphibious sort of animal, having fourteen times crossed the
ocean, in furtherance of colonial enterprise. At home—if that phrase can be
used of one so ubiquitous—he is the Joseph Hume of the Legislative Council,
and Tribune of the People in public meetings, in addition to his labours in
the Pulpit or the Press. To his labours must be added his sufferings, for he
not long ago spent a month within the walls of a prison. Having now
declared for a Republic, he probably means to finish off by being its first
President ! We gather these particulars from his own narrative. So inge-
nuous a man excites our sympathy. It is right to add, that his imprisonment
was for libel ; and in this respect, it is marvellous how his Ishmaelitish nature
escaped the fangs of the law so long. As it is, he seems to be never " out of
hot water''; and not the least amusing part of these volumes is the account of
his endless litigations. Of course he is always in the right ; and we are not
disposed to question this, although his talents, we think, might have been
better employed. He manifests great practical genius—at least, he can lay
down a practical scheme ; and he only fails in successfully executing it, for
want of that co-operation which his temper renders impossible. We say
this in justice to Dr. Lang's really honest character and honorable purposes ;
and we believe this to be really a more reasonable way of accounting for

failures for which he has been loudly blamed, than to suppose him guilty of deliberately imposing on an unsuspecting public. Our respect is due to any man who has toiled for years in the public service, and spent his own uttermost farthing in single-handed endeavours to promote great public ends. He complains much of misrepresentation. But what can he expect, considering the numerous public men who are dragged into almost every page of his work, and loaded with the most scurrilous abuse ?

"Of the two volumes, the first is 'historical,' and the second 'statistical.' They are both characterized by the faults referred to, but they are, nevertheless, of great value, the latter especially. Its topographical and industrial information is very minute and practical. It should be read by every intelligent emigrant, and by all who would form a correct conception of the resources of a country at one time thought to be only a continent of sheep-runs. Its adaptation for vine and cotton cultivation is specially exhibited. The fact admits of no doubt, and in future years these productions will be a source of wealth to their cultivators ; but, in urging the immediate practicability of competing with the American cotton-planters, Dr. Lang has either forgotten the diggings, or neglected to revise a statement written at a previous date, when he contends that free labour in Australia is as cheap as slave labour in America. This is no longer the real state of the case."

The *Eclectic Review*, in one of its " Brief Notices," thus summed up Dr. Lang's historical merits on the same occasion :—

"Few men are so competent to detail the history of Australian emigration. A residence of many years in this distant Colony, unwearied activity both of mind and body, frequent intercourse with the officials, much shrewdness and force of character, and an intimate knowledge of, and personal share in, many of the most important transactions, pre-eminently qualify Dr. Lang to be the historian of New South Wales. On the other hand, it must be admitted that the strength of his antipathies—the fierce vehemence of his dislikes—is sadly in the way of impartiality. This is specially seen in the tenth chapter of his first volume. We fear there is too much truth in it, but, true or false, it shakes confidence in the coolness and impartiality of the historian, and wakens the mistrust with which we regard statements made in self-defence. The colouring of this part of the work is that of a controversial pamphlet, rather than of a history, which we much regret. But notwithstanding this grave deduction, we strongly recommend the volumes to our friends. They constitute the ablest and most interesting history we possess

K

of this vast dependency, and open up many points of colonial government on which the English public need to be informed. Of the author's integrity there is no doubt, and his means of information have been most ample."

1846.—A HISTORY OF NEW SOUTH WALES, *from its Settlement to the close of the year* 1844. By T. H. Braim, Esq., Principal of Sydney College. London. 2 vols., 8vo.

The historical portion of this work is by no means full, and in that respect it is not to be compared with either Lang's or Flanagan's. The most important events in our annals, however, are all comprised in a brief sketch of the various Administrations. A great deal of attention is paid to the subjects of Emigration, the abuses of the Convict System, the Land Laws, the Religious and Educational Establishments. There is also a lengthy analysis of the proceedings of the first representative Council, during 1843 and 1844. "The plan upon which the following work is composed," says the author, "is of a descriptive as well as statistical nature, combining the mode and style pursued by Lang and Martin. It has always appeared to us that the former is too generally descriptive, the latter too sterile in his materials, for general interest. Lang is exceedingly meagre in his statistical details, and weak in his financial views; Martin is replete with figures, but such as are often incorrect and sometimes contradictory."

Mr. Braim's style is rhapsodical, and his religious sympathies are very strong. The latter part of his work is rather of a " Stranger's Guide to Sydney" character; and although interesting at the present day, as an illustration of our progress, is hardly appropriate in a History. In this respect the work resembles Mr. Wentworth's. It is not entitled to be termed a History; it is simply a "statistical, historical, and political account" of the Colony. Nevertheless, it constitutes a valuable contribution to our historical literature.

1855.—AUSTRALIA AND ITS GOLD FIELDS : *an Historical Sketch of the progress of the Australian Colonies, from the earliest times to the present day; with a particular account of the recent Gold Discoveries, and observations on the present aspect of the Land Question : to which are added, notices on the use and working of Gold in ancient and modern times ; and an examination of the Theories as to the source of Gold.* By E. H. Hargraves, late Commissioner of Crown Lands in New South Wales. London. 8vo. pages.

Two chapters in this book are interesting. They detail the author's experience as a gold miner in California, in 1850—the circumstances under which he was led to believe, while there, that Australia was also a gold-bearing country—his return to New South Wales—his search for the precious metal—and his success. The other chapters were apparently added to make up a book ; and it is said that Mr. Hargraves was materially assisted in their composition.

The question as to the first discovery of gold in this country has excited a good deal of controversy. Mr. Hargraves speaks of the respective claims of Sir Roderick Murchison and the Rev. W. B. Clarke. Without any pretension to geological knowledge himself, he yet undertakes to ridicule the title of the latter gentleman to the honour of this discovery. It should be observed that, although there is no doubt as to Mr. Hargraves having been the first to *proclaim* the existence of gold in this country, his statements require to be read in connection with those of another author on this subject—Mr. Davison.

Mr. Hargraves describes the excited state of his feelings on actually finding gold. Conscious that he was about to work a revolution in the country, he exclaimed to his guide :—" This is a memorable day in the history of New South Wales. I shall be a baronet, you will be knighted, and my old horse will be stuffed, put into a glass case, and sent to the British Museum"!

1860.—THE DISCOVERY AND GEOGNOSY OF GOLD DEPOSITS IN AUSTRALIA; *with comparisons and accounts of the Gold Regions in California, Russia, India, Brazil, &c.; including a philosophical disquisition on the Origin of Gold in Placer-Deposits, and in Quartz Veins.* By Simpson Davison, Member of the Philosophical Society of New South Wales, and late Mining Associate of the Gold Discoverer recognized by the local Government, and employed as Crown Commissioner for Exploration of Gold Fields in Australia. Illustrated with Chromo-tinted Map. London. 8vo., 482 pages.

The author of this valuable work came to this Colony in 1844, in quest of fortune and adventure. He lived for some years in various parts of the interior, as a squatter, and thus had considerable opportunities of studying the geological character of the country. He had been interested in geological studies from a very early age; and although he does not pretend to the character of a professional geologist, he is evidently a master of the science. Not having met with much success on his stations, he determined to take a trip to California, at that time the great centre of attraction. He sailed in 1849, and spent three years upon the mines in that country. One of his fellow passengers from Sydney was Mr. Hargraves, whose book has just been mentioned. They became partners in gold mining, and lived together during the whole time of the latter's stay. Mr. Hargraves returned to New South Wales at the close of the year 1850, and Mr. Davison followed about two years after.

The object of this book is to shew that Mr. Hargraves is *not* entitled to the credit of the Australian Gold Discovery. The author states that, while on his stations in the north and south of this Colony, he had attentively examined the geological structure of the country; that while in California, he also attentively examined the geological structure of the mining districts; and that he formed the conclusion, from a comparison of the two, that gold existed in New South Wales. He further states that this conclusion was imparted to his companion, Mr. Hargraves, who knew nothing of geology, and was not given to attentive examinations of a geological character; and that when Mr. Hargraves was about to return to Sydney, he strongly advised him to search at once for gold on his arrival there, and told him the precise spots in which to search for it. Now, Mr. Hargraves, in his book, says little or nothing on this subject. He gives no credit to Mr. Davison for even a hint upon it. On the contrary, he asserts that his conclusions with respect to Australian gold were entirely original—that, from first to last, he, and he only, was "The Australian Gold Discoverer."

Mr. Davison's book is certainly a far superior one to that of Mr. Hargraves, being the production of an educated and an able man. It is a valuable contribution to the History of the Colony, inasmuch as it comprises every particular relating to the Gold Discovery.

1862.—THE HISTORY OF NEW SOUTH WALES ; *with an account of Van Diemen's Land [Tasmania], New Zealand, Port Phillip [Victoria], Moreton Bay, and other Australasian Settlements : comprising a complete View of the Progress and Prospects of Gold Mining in Australia. The whole compiled from official and other authentic and original sources.* By Roderick Flanagan, Member of the Australian Literary Institute, and of the Philosophical Society of New South Wales. London, 2 vols., 8vo.

This work is carefully compiled, and forms a very trustworthy source of information. The author has availed himself largely of official records, and has thus succeeded in giving an accurate outline of Australian History. He has confined himself, in a great measure, to a simple detail of the leading facts comprised in that history. He has not sought to amplify his materials by philosophising upon them, or to enliven them by the colouring of imagination. The work is perhaps as free from prejudice as any work of the kind can be expected to be. In his preface, the author modestly restricts his merits to those of "zeal and application." They cannot certainly be denied him, for there is evidence of industry in every page. The book, however, cannot be considered a well-written one. Mr. Flanagan's style of writing is rather heavy.

The following notice of this elaborate compilation appeared in the chapter on "Contemporary Literature" in the *Westminster Review* :—

"To furnish a connected narrative of the affairs of New South Wales, from the period when the country first came under the notice of Europeans to the present time, has been the object which Mr. Flanagan has proposed to himself in his comprehensive and laborious history. Commencing, after a brief preliminary retrospect, with the voyage of the first fleet, he traces the progress of events under which the colonists have achieved their ultimate prosperity, describes the difficulties which attended the first settlement of a remote territory ; the enterprise displayed in the work of discovery and exploration ; the successful struggle of a daughter-people to introduce into a new country the free institutions which their ancestors had conquered for them. In general, Mr. Flanagan's narrative is very full. Compiled from official and newspaper sources, it is, however, naturally somewhat heavy—the style possesses no attraction—and the principal interest of the story arises from the relation of a British Colony to the Mother Country. Mr. Flanagan is not a philosopher. His work has no ethnological element. We can find in it little about the natives worth reporting."

1863.—Reminiscences of Thirty Years' Residence in New South Wales and Victoria ; *with a Supplementary Chapter on Transportation and the Ticket-of-leave System.* By R. Therry, Esq., late one of the Judges of the Supreme Court of New South Wales. London. 8vo., 514 pages.

Mr. Therry has thrown together a large number of interesting details in this volume, many of which are valuable as historical illustrations. The various positions he occupied in this Colony gave him many opportunities for acquiring information, and a work of some solid pretensions might have been expected from his pen. In this, however, he disappointed his readers. He committed the strange mistake of reviving the memory of crimes long since forgotten, and thus excited a very bitter style of criticism towards himself. That this was not done with the purpose of giving pain he sufficiently proved by suppressing the book.

1866.—The History of Australian Discovery and Colonization.

This work is not yet completed. It is published in single chapters in the *Empire*, and republished in parts, four of which have already appeared. The history of the Colony has been brought down to the administration of Governor Darling, which lasted from 1825 to 1831. In more than one respect, this is the best of our historical productions. It is well written; it is full and accurate in its details; and it is free from prejudice or party feeling. It comprehends, moreover, an exact account of the progress of Australian discovery and exploration. This portion of our History has been done by the Rev. Mr. Woods, in his "History of Australian Discovery and Exploration," and it has also been sketched in other works on these Colonies; but there is no full account of it in any History of New South Wales, besides the one we are now noticing. The author has not confined himself to mere details of public transactions, but has endeavoured to illustrate the social progress of the community. The following passage is an instance :—

"The choice of Campbelltown as the place at which to hold the first assizes was more owing to the fact that a very large number of wealthy families had estates in the surrounding districts, and that many daring acts of bushranging had taken place there, than to the importance of the township itself. The discovery, not long after the first settlement of the Colony, of the rich lands of the Cowpastures, Camden, the Valleys of Bunbury Curran, Mulgoa, and other tracts of fertile soil, made that district a favourite one with the more influential colonists; and it was there that many of them, having secured extensive grants of land, had settled with their families and formed their homesteads. Their residences were, in many instances, places of far more than ordinary pretensions; some of them indeed were mansions almost rivalling "the stately homes of England" in cost, extent, and appearance. Many non-resident colonists also possessed estates there on which they had numerous tenants and labourers. Some few of these estates still remain the property of the families or descendants of the original grantees; but most of them, in the sharp reverses of colonial life, have long since passed into the hands of strangers, and having been cut up and subdivided into lots, have been sold and resold under the hammer of the auctioneer, until their identity is almost lost. They were named, in some instances, after the ancient seats of noble or wealthy families in the old country; in others they bore the name of a commander or a ship under whom, or in which, the original grantee or some progenitor had served. Some told of battles in which the owner or his ancestors had taken part, and some of far-off native villages or hamlets. A few retained the beautifully expressive and sonorous aboriginal names; but hardly in a single instance did the old colonists outrage good taste, and render themselves and the country ridiculous, by conferring such stupid appellations as have lately prevailed in colonial nomenclature. These early colonists, indeed, to their honor be it spoken, in bestowing names upon their estates, appear to have acted under the elevating ideas that they were not only the founders of families, but were helping to create " a new Britannia in another world"; and hence their nomenclature was almost always racy of the great country from which they had come, and with whose glories they wished to identify themselves and their posterity. It is true that their hopes of becoming the founders of wealthy families were in few cases fully realized; but their ambition was not an ignoble one, and it would have been well for some of their descendants of the present generation if they had inherited more of the sentiments of their fathers. A few of the names of the families settled or possessing estates within the distance of twenty or thirty miles of Campbelltown, and whose members doubtless formed part of the numerous cavalcade which welcomed to that place the first Judge and barristers that ever went on circuit in Australia, will tend to illustrate the preceding remarks. There were the Macarthurs, Macleays, and Cowpers, of Camden, Camden Park, and Wivenhoe; the Oxleys, Coghills, Harringtons, and

Hawdons, of Kirkham, Elderslie, and Malton; the Howes, of Glenlee and Eskdale; the Rileys, of Ousedale and Rahy; Brooks, of Denham Court; Throsby, of Glenfield and Smeaton; Broughton, of Lachlan Vale; Cordeaux, of Leppington; Wylde, of Cecil Park; Wills, of Varroville; Hassall, of Macquarie Grove; Jamison, of Cowdeknaws; Molle, of Netherby; Blaxland, of Ludenham; the Coxes and Shadforths, of Winborne, Fernhill, and Clarendon; the Campbells, of Harrington Park and Shancamore; the Antills, of Picton; the Savages, of Claremont; the Wentworths, of Elmshall Park and Vermont; the Humes, of Hillshorough, Brookdale, and Hume Wood; Brown, of Oakham; Lowe, of Birling; Jones, of Fleurs; Judge Bent's estate was called Wolverton; Judge Field's was Hinchinbrook—all these, and many more with similar old country or suggestive names, were within an easy distance of the place fixed upon as the assize town, where no doubt their possessors fondly hoped that during a long series of years they—the landed gentry of that part of the Colony—would assemble at the assize ball, in imitation of the old country usage, by which annual gatherings of fair women and brave men are made to give *éclat* to the visits of the ministers of justice, social observances are invoked in aid of order, and local influence is exercised to uphold the dignity of the judicial office. The houses of many of the more wealthy resident settlers in the district referred to were designed, and some of them actually built, on a scale which, with reference to the remoteness of the Colony and the circumstances by which they were surrounded, may he fitly described as magnificent; but there were other estates, with high-sounding names, where nothing better in the shape of buildings than aggregations of hark huts were to he found. The hopes of many had heen disappointed and their plans frustrated hy the financial disasters previously referred to. Castles in the air had suddenly faded, and the day dreams of intending founders of families had heen rudely interrupted by the entry of the sheriff's officer. The fluctuating circumstances by which colonial existence is surrounded, have always proved fatal sooner or later to the designs of those who have endeavoured to found a territorial aristocracy. But although this result is undoubtedly upon the whole favourable to the progress and prosperity of new communities, it is often accompanied by circumstances which even the most ardent republican or democrat cannot but regard with regret. An ever-shifting population, with no ties to hind it to the soil, where there are few spots consecrated by the associations and memories of home, can never hecome a nation. The privileged or fortunate few who, in the infancy of Australian colonization, obtained large tracts of freehold land, aimed at the founding of homes around which their descendants for many generations might be expected to cluster, and where, amidst tenants, retainers, and dependents, would grow up a condition of things bearing a close resemblance to that in which the landed aristocracy of England is placed. Although it was doubtless fortunate for the many that the hopes of the few were disappointed, it is impossible to repress a feeling of regret that designs and aspirations partaking of so much that was noble and elevating should have been so completely frustrated. The pride of race—the consciousness of high social standing—the sentiment of family antiquity—however absurd when carried to excess, are capable of exercising, if kept under proper control, a very restraining and refining influence upon individual character. This influence is almost or altogether absent where the population is constantly fluctuating, where there are few permanently settled families, and where, to use an expressive colloquialism, 'Jack is as good as his master.' The Campbelltown of to-day bears few indications that forty years since it attained to the dignity of an assize town ; the seats of many of the once numerous gentry of the district, long ago deserted by their original owners, have in most instances fallen into decay ; and the farms—reduced to modest proportions—are occupied by tenants or peasant proprietors."

BIOGRAPHY.

1854.—DIARY OF A VISIT TO ENGLAND, IN 1776, by an Irish-
man (The Reverend Dr. Thomas Campbell, Author of "A
Philosophical Survey of the South of Ireland"); and other
Papers, by the same hand. With Notes, by Samuel Raymond,
M.A., Prothonotary of the Supreme Court of New South
Wales. Sydney. 8vo., 167 pages.

The Diary published by Mr. Raymond was discovered by a
Clerk of the Supreme Court, "behind an old press, which had not
been moved for years." The author, Dr. Campbell, was a learned
Irishman, who, on the occasion of his visit to England, gained the
acquaintance of Dr. Johnson and other celebrities of the time.
His name occurs more than once in Boswell's Life of Johnson.
How his manuscript Diary found its way into an office of the
Supreme Court in Sydney, was a mystery which the editor was
unable to solve. An article in the *Edinburgh Review* supplied a
clue which was followed up successfully by a reviewer in the
Sydney Morning Herald. In vol. vii of Nichol's " Literary Illustrations" occurs a passage with respect to the " eldest nephew
and heir" of Dr. Campbell, by name John Thomas Campbell.
It is there stated that the latter was on his way, in 1810, to New
South Wales, in the hope of procuring some Government appointment in the Colony. The reviewer in the *Herald*, on searching
the files of the *Gazette*, discovered that John Thomas Campbell
filled the two offices of Provost Marshal and Colonial Secretary
until the year 1821, when he was appointed Sheriff and Provost
Marshal. In this capacity, he no doubt had an office in the
Supreme Court, and in this office he must have left the manuscript
of his literary uncle. The book is one of the " Curiosities of
Literature," and its contents are extremely interesting. The
editor has appended a large amount of information in the shape
of " Addenda."

1855.—Memoirs, Historical and Scientific, of the Right Honourable Sir Joseph Banks, Bart., D.C.L., *of the University of Oxford, and more than forty years President of the Royal Society of London, and Member of the National Institute of Paris, &c., &c., &c.* By George Suttor, F.L.S., of London. Parramatta. 8vo., 80 pages.

Mr. Suttor was sent out to this Colony as a botanical collector, through the interest of Sir Joseph Banks. He speaks in the highest terms of admiration of his distinguished patron; and although his language is that of an uneducated man, the " Memoirs" abound in interesting details. The book contains, as an appendix, the *Eloge Historique de Sir Joseph Banks*, pronounced by the President of the National Institute of France, Cuvier, on the death of the great naturalist.

1857.—The Life, Experience, and Journal of Nathaniel Pidgeon, City Missionary. Written by himself. Sydney. 8vo., 223 pages.

This little book has no pretensions to literary merit, but it is interesting as the record of a zealous City Missionary. The illustrations it affords of the mental workings of an enthusiast, of the scenes which take place in the lowest classes of society, and of the practical operation of religion among them, render it highly interesting in a psychological point of view.

1864.—The Confessions of Wavering Worthy; or, The Great Secret of Success in Life; *an Ethical and Autobiographical Essay.* Edited by his most intimate friend, E. Wardley, M.R.C.S.L., and inscribed to the rising generation of Australia, by the Author. Sydney. 8vo., 261 pages.

In this work the author has given us a minute dissection of his own character, accompanied by abundant personal details, for the purpose of pointing out the cause of his want of success in life.

He describes himself as a dreamy, irresolute, imaginative man, unable to avail himself of any opportunity for "getting on" in the world, and passing on, from one stage of his existence to another, without making the slightest effort to control surrounding circumstances to his own advantage. Having qualified himself for the medical profession, and yet done nothing to obtain a practice, he came to this Colony in 1853. Here he appeared in a variety of characters before the world, but none of them proved a "hit." He first became a gold-digger—then a country doctor—then a lounger about town—then he occupied himself on a farm—and at last settled down in the Government service. In many cases he has described his sufferings and experiences with a very graphic pen; his sketch of a country doctor, for instance, is irresistible. These portions of the work are by far the most valuable. The "ethical" disquisitions are not calculated to interest the reader. With reference to this subject, it may be noted that he describes his failure throughout life as the result of lurking insanity, and then proceeds to give a series of remarkable cases that have occurred within his experience as a medical officer in a lunatic asylum. This idea is apparently started for the purpose of introducing these illustrations of insanity, for the author gives no reason for attributing madness to himself. His case is a common one, being that of a man of some power, neutralized by want of will and energy. Throughout the work the author has scattered a variety of pieces in verse, which do more, perhaps, to illustrate his own character than anything else he has written. One of these pieces, "The Two Sisters," has some merit. He is not always happy in his style, being much too diffuse, and altogether wanting in epigrammatic expression. No one can read it, however, without a feeling of esteem for its author, as an accomplished, amiable, and much-enduring man, who deserved a better fate than he has met with, and who has done his best to make his own experience a guiding light to others.

TRAVELS AND VOYAGES.

1820.—JOURNALS OF TWO EXPEDITIONS INTO THE INTERIOR OF
NEW SOUTH WALES, *undertaken by order of the British
Government, in the years* 1817–18. By John Oxley, *Surveyor
General of the Territory, and Lieutenant of the Royal Navy.*
With Maps and Views of the interior and newly discovered
country. London. 4to.

This volume represents the third important step in the progress of exploration. The object of Mr. Oxley's expeditions was
to trace, as far as practicable, the Macquarie and Lachlan Rivers,
discovered by Mr. Evans, a surveyor, with a view to ascertain
the character of the country through which they flowed. In
1817, Mr. Oxley followed the course of the Lachlan until it was
lost in successive marshes. In 1818, he traced the Macquarie
in the same manner, and met with the same result. Mr. Oxley
concluded that the interior of the country was an immense swamp,
and that these rivers, as well as a third, the Castlereagh, lost
themselves in it. This remained, for some time, the prevailing
opinion as to the character of the interior.

1823.—A JOURNAL OF A TOUR OF DISCOVERY ACROSS THE BLUE
MOUNTAINS IN NEW SOUTH WALES. By G. Blaxland.
London. 12mo., 48 pages.

This was the first successful attempt to penetrate across the
" Blue Mountains" into the interior. A belief had generally
prevailed among the first settlers that these mountains were
impassable. Captain Sturt tells us that " a Mr. Caley is said to
have been the first who attempted to scale the Blue Mountains;
but he did not long persevere in struggling with difficulties too
great for ordinary resolution to overcome. It appears that he
retraced his steps, after having penetrated about sixteen miles

into their dark and precipitous recesses; and a heap of stones, which the traveller passes about that distance from Erne Ford, on the road to Bathurst, marks the extreme point reached by the first Expedition to the westward of the Nepean River." The occurrence of a protracted drought, however, rendered it necessary to overcome this difficulty in the path. A second expedition was successful. Messrs. Wentworth, Lawson, and Blaxland, attended by four servants, and four horses laden with provisions, started on the 11th May, 1813, from Mr. Blaxland's farm at the South Creek. They crossed the mountains, and returned home on the 6th of June following. "The achievement of this undertaking," says the author of "The History of Australian Colonisation and Discovery," "was the commencement of a new era in the history of the Colony. No longer confined to the comparatively barren strip of coast land to the east of the mountains, the settlers acquired fresh vigour as they found their prospects expanding, and saw the great plains of the interior thrown open to their occupation. It is from this time that the real prosperity of the Colony dates."

1837.— Journey of Discovery to Port Phillip, New South
Wales, in 1824 and 1825. By W. H. Hovell and H. Hume,
Esquires. Second Edition. Sydney. 8vo., 97 pages.

Among the various explorations of the Colony, it would be difficult to mention any that could be described as either more important or more interesting than this. Its object was to ascertain the truth of the conclusions arrived at by Mr. Oxley, the Surveyor General, as to the character of the interior. The Expedition—like that of Messrs. Wentworth, Lawson, and Blaxland—was a private one. It was eminently successful. It demonstrated the existence of immense tracts of country, covered with grass, and adapted both to grazing and to agriculture. The dismal theory of the Surveyor General was blown to the winds, and the prospects of the country seemed fairer than ever.

The account of this expedition, mentioned above, was edited by Dr. Bland, an old and patriotic colonist. It would not be readily supposed that such a publication could possibly involve a bitter public dissension. Even in 1837, however, society was so constituted in Sydney that the editing a simple statement was regarded as a strong political demonstration. A public official had declared that the interior of New Holland was a barren desert, and all the ranks of officialism immediately echoed the cry. Two private gentlemen proved that the interior was well grassed, well watered, and only required to be well populated in order to rival the fat meadows of an English landscape. The question was contested with all the furious intolerance of a theological dispute in the sixteenth century. The story is well told in the "History of Australian Discovery and Colonisation":—

"The accounts of their journey given by Messrs. Hume and Hovell gave rise to great discussion, and to no small amount of ill-feeling and recrimination between the dominating or official class and the rest of the colonists. The former, acting with their usual *esprit de corps*, took the part of the Surveyor General against the private explorers, whose claims, on the other hand, were loudly endorsed by the general public. There was perhaps a tendency on one side, arising from violent party feeling, unduly to decry the services of Mr. Oxley. In justice to that gentleman, it ought to be stated that he had been persevering, and to a great extent successful, in his explorations; but the mistaken theories he had broached relative to the south and south-western interior laid him open to animadversion, and gave party animosity a fair ground for reproach. It is almost impossible now to enter fully into the feelings which prompted the leaders of both sections of the colonists to make a violent dispute about a subject apparently so far removed from social or political differences as the character of the then almost unknown interior; or to understand thoroughly that condition of society where the claims of men who had rendered great services to the community were sought to be ignored, because their recognition was supposed to cast some reflection on a mere theory or opinion broached by an official. So strong was this feeling, however, in the case of Messrs. Hume and Hovell, that when, a few days after their return, they attended the annual meeting at Parramatta of the New South Wales Agricultural Society (an association whose management was under the influence of the official class), all allusion to them or their achievement was carefully suppressed in the programme of after-dinner speeches, while the Surveyor General's explorations were spoken of in terms of fulsome eulogy. And so strong and enduring was this feeling of jealousy on the part of the dominant clique, that when, several years afterwards, Dr. Bland edited the account of Messrs. Hume and Hovell's journey, and pointed out the errors into which the Surveyor General had fallen, he was thought to have done a very bold thing."

1837.—VOYAGE TO TORRES' STRAIT, in search of the Survivors of the ship "*Charles Eaton*," in the Colonial schooner "*Isabella*," C. M. Lewis, commander. By Capt. King, R.N. Sydney. 8vo.

1838.—THREE EXPEDITIONS INTO THE INTERIOR OF EASTERN AUSTRALIA, WITH DESCRIPTIONS OF THE RECENTLY EXPLORED REGION OF AUSTRALIA FELIX, AND OF THE PRESENT COLONY OF NEW SOUTH WALES. By Major T. L. Mitchell, F.G.S. and M.R.G.S., Surveyor General. London. 2 vols., 8vo.

The first of these expeditions (1831-2) originated in the report of a captured bushranger that a large river called the " Kindur" existed in the north-west, by following which he had twice reached the sea-shore. The result of Mitchell's exploration was that no such river could be found. The bushranger's story was an invention.

The second expedition (1835) was formed for the purpose of exploring the course of the River Darling. Soon after they started, Mr. Richard Cunningham, the botanist, lost his way in the bush, and was never seen again. The narrative is deeply affecting, and vividly recalls the peculiar dangers of the Australian bush. The Expedition was not altogether a success. Major Mitchell traced the Darling for many miles, ascertained that it was chiefly supported by springs, and made known the junction of the Bogan and the Darling.

The third Expedition is one of the most memorable in the annals of exploration. It resulted in the discovery of Australia Felix, or, as it is now called, Victoria. The country over which Major Mitchell led his party appeared the richest and most beautiful he had ever seen. A succession of views burst upon their eyes that would have enchanted a party of Royal Academicians in the search for the picturesque. At one time, for instance, they came upon a valley, which is thus described by Mitchell :— "I had not proceeded more than about five miles to the south, when I perceived before me a ridge in the bluey distance, which was rather an unusual object in that close country. We soon emerged from the ridge, and found that we were on a kind of table-land, and approaching a deep ravine coming from our right, terminating in a fine open country below, watered by a winding river. We descended to the bottom of the ravine, and found there a foaming little river hurrying downwards over the rocks. After this, we ascended a very steep but grassy mountain-side beyond it; and, on reaching a brow of high land, what a noble prospect appeared! a river winding among meadows, fully a mile broad, and green as an emerald. Above them rose swelling hills of fantastic shapes, but all were smooth and richly covered with grass. Behind these were higher hills, having grass on their sides, and trees on their summits, extending throughout the landscape as far as the eye could reach, forming a country surpassing in beauty and richness any yet discovered." This was the vale of the Wannon.

Few books are more attractive than these journals of our explorers, notwithstanding the want of polish in their style, and too often the monotony of their contents. There is no absence of dramatic incident, while the scenes described are frequently interesting in the extreme. Major Mitchell tells his reader that "The following journals were written at the close of many a laborious day, when the energies both of mind and body were almost exhausted by long continued toil." Under such circumstances, we do not expect a finished literary composition. Dr. Lang found it impossible to balance his sentences while engaged in balancing himself in stormy weather at sea. The difficulties of composition could hardly be less when undertaken in the tent of an explorer.

Major Mitchell's works are additionally valuable from the large amount of scientific information they contain. He was an acute observer, and nothing of interest escaped him. In the preface to this work, he alludes to "another task, of a national character," on which he was engaged—*Plans of the Fields of Battle in the Peninsula.*

1848.—Journal of an Expedition into the Interior of Tropical Australia, *in search of a Route from Sydney to the Gulf of Carpentaria.* By Lieut.-Col. Sir T. L. Mitchell, Knight, D.C.L., *Surveyor General of New South Wales.* London. 8vo.

The author states the object of this expedition to have been the discovery of a practicable route from Sydney to the Gulf of Carpentaria, for the purpose of facilitating trade with India and China, and communication with England. It did not succeed in penetrating to the Gulf, but a large portion of the northern interior was laid open, and discoveries of great importance were the result. These related principally to the river system of the north. The Maranoa, Belyando, and Victoria Rivers, were made known to the colonists, together with the splendid country through which they flowed. Sir Thomas Mitchell is neither a very eloquent nor a very graphic writer, and his pages are encumbered with the technicalities of botany, but his journal is highly interesting nevertheless. He is a warm friend, if not an enthusiastic admirer, of the aboriginals. He explains the manner in which their cruelties towards defenceless white men have been provoked, and he maintains that they are by no means deficient in intelligence. The volume is well illustrated, and contains many passages of striking interest. None of our explorers, unfortunately, have possessed much power of word-painting, and consequently their publications are by no means so graphic as they might have been.

[No date.]—THE LAST CRUISE OF THE *Wanderer*. By John Webster. Sydney. 8vo., 128 pages.

The *Wanderer* was a yacht belonging to Mr. Benjamin Boyd, who sailed in her on a cruise from San Francisco to the Hawaiian Islands. The object of the expedition is stated, in the preface, to have been the establishment, in the Islands of the Pacific, of "a Papuan Republic or Confederation : to lay the foundation of some sort of social and political organisation, on which the simple machinery of an independent State might be afterwards erected." Mr. Boyd met with a fate very similar to that of Captain Cook. Having landed one morning on an island off which his yacht was at anchor, he was never seen again, and the inference of course was, that he was set upon and murdered ; while shortly afterwards the yacht was attacked by a large number of savages in their canoes, and his crew narrowly escaped the fate of their leader. Mr. Boyd was a gentleman well known in this Colony, where he had previously spent many years of his life. His death excited a general feeling of regret and commiseration. The writer of the narrative was a friend of his who, with others, had joined the expedition from a love of adventure. The account of the voyage, and of the various islands they arrived at, with their picturesque scenery, is extremely interesting. The volume, it may be added, is handsomely printed.

1849.—Narrative of an Expedition undertaken under the direction of the late Mr. Assistant Surveyor E. B. Kennedy, for the exploration of the Country lying between Rockingham Bay and Cape York. By W. Carron, one of the survivors of the Expedition. *To which are added*—(1) *The statement of the aboriginal native, Jackey Jackey, who accompanied Mr. Kennedy* ; (2) *The statement of Dr. Vallack and Captn. Dobson, who rescued the survivors of the Expedition ; and* (3) *The statement of Captn. Simpson, of the " Freak," who proceeded in search of Mr. Kennedy's papers.* Sydney. 8vo.

The expedition commanded by Mr. Kennedy was the most disastrous that ever attempted to explore the interior of this country. Of thirteen men who started, three only returned. They survived a series of sufferings that is almost incredible.

Mr. Kennedy had accompanied Sir Thomas Mitchell on some of his expeditions. Being practically acquainted with the dangers and the difficulties of exploration, he was selected to take command of a party for the purpose of opening a route from Sydney to the northern coast. There existed at the time a strong desire among the people of this country to establish a means of communication with the north. Any practicable route across the continent would enable them to monopolize the trade with the East Indies, and thus to maintain their rank as the oldest and wealthiest of these Colonies. Mr. Kennedy's expedition was despatched to accomplish this object. The design was, to explore the east side of Carpentaria, and ascertain the character of the country about Cape York. They were to proceed by sea to Rockingham Bay, land there, and make their way across the peninsula to Port Albany.

The pathos of this simple narrative could hardly be excelled. From the first, the party was beset with such difficulties that success appeared impossible. They had to cut their way through almost impenetrable scrub. They had to cross deep ravines, climb precipitous mountains, stumble over rocky plains, and ward off the spears of hostile savages. Soon their provisions failed them. They had to depend upon horseflesh. Some of the party fell ill, and were unable to move. At length, the leader resolved to break up the party. He left some behind in camp, and pushed on with the rest. He had not gone far when it was necessary to repeat this process. He then started with the blackfellow, Jackey Jackey, who had been their companion from the first. They were pursued by the aboriginals. A spear hit him on the back. The barb was no sooner cut out by Jackey Jackey, than another spear struck him, above the knee. He struggled on, but at last was obliged to lie down. He tried to write, but his strength was gone, and falling back in the arms of Jackey Jackey, he breathed his last.

1855.—A BRIEF STATEMENT OF FACTS IN CONNECTION WITH AN OVERLAND EXPEDITION FROM LAKE GEORGE TO PORT PHILLIP, IN 1824. By Hamilton Hume. Edited by the Rev. W. Ross, Goulburn. Sydney. 8vo., 34 pages.

The purport of this statement is to shew how far the success of the Expedition was due to Mr. Hume, and how far to his companion, Mr. Hovell. On many public occasions the credit of the enterprise was given to the latter, and Mr. Hume's share in it apparently forgotten. Hurt by this injustice, Mr. Hume judged it expedient to put on record the true history of the Expedition, and, by that means, to shew that its success was almost entirely owing to his own exertions. He says, in his introduction, " I hope it may not be imputed as unwarranted or discreditable that I have felt roused, and somewhat chagrined, to find that Mr. Hovell has almost monopolized with the public the fame and credit of the Expedition to Port Phillip, in which he was associated with myself, in 1824 ; and that where my name has been referred to at all, it has almost invariably been in a secondary style, and more as Mr. Hovell's companion or assistant, than as the 'undertaker and leader of the Expedition.'"

This case of *tulit alter honores* affords a striking parallel to that of the gold discovery. In each instance, all the honor and profit of the venture seem to have been borne away by one who possessed rather luck than merit.

1865.—WAYFARING NOTES : *Sydney to Southampton, by way of Egypt and Palestine.* Printed for private distribution. Sydney. 8vo., 340 pages.

The author of this work—the contents of which originally appeared in the *Herald*—is Professor Smith, of the University. It contains some graphic descriptions, and is principally occupied with the details of a voyage up the Nile, and an account of the tombs of Egypt. The antiquities of the Holy Land are also minutely noted. The narrative is not equal to Eliot Warburton's, but it is highly interesting, nevertheless.

PHILOLOGY.

1827.—SPECIMENS OF A DIALECT OF THE ABORIGINES OF NEW SOUTH WALES, *being the first attempt to form their Speech into a written Language.* By L. E. Threlkeld. Sydney. [Out of print.]

1834.—AN AUSTRALIAN GRAMMAR, *comprehending the principles and natural rules of the Language, as spoken by the Aborigines in the vicinity of Hunter's River, Lake Macquarie, &c., New South Wales.* By L. E. Threlkeld. Sydney. 8vo.

1850.—A KEY TO THE STRUCTURE OF THE ABORIGINAL LANGUAGE; *being an analysis of the particles used as affixes to form the various modifications of the Verbs; shewing the essential powers, abstract roots, and other peculiarities of the Language spoken by the Aborigines in the vicinity of Hunter's River, Lake Macquarie, &c., New South Wales; together with a comparison of Polynesian and other Dialects.* By L. E. Threlkeld. Sydney. 8vo.

Mr. Threlkeld was a laborious and enthusiastic Missionary among the savage tribes of Otaheite and Australia, for a period of nearly twenty years. The works mentioned above display a perfect acquaintance with the subject they profess to treat, and form a highly respectable contribution to the science of Philology.

The aboriginals of this country are divided, as usually happens among savage races, into many distinct tribes, each tribe having its own dialect. These dialects, however, are so different from each other that it would be more correct to term them languages. Mr. Threlkeld's book treats only one portion of the general subject; that is to say, it is confined to the dialects of the tribes residing in a certain district of the Colony. Within its own limits, it appears to be as correct as it could be well expected.

His literary labours did not end here. In a letter from his pen, published in a colonial magazine, in 1857, it is stated that, "The Gospel of Luke, in the aboriginal language, is completed in manuscript; besides which, there is now in progress a Lexicon, to accompany it, of the Australian and English, containing an explanation of the letters, words, and phrases, occurring in the Gospel of Luke, and will be shortly ready for publication. The native blacks are so rapidly becoming extinct, that the language must of necessity, unless preserved by the functions of the Press, become utterly lost to posterity." I have not been able to find either of the works mentioned here.

1856.—GURRE KAMILAROI: *or, Kamilaroi Sayings.* By William Ridley, Missionary; with Illustrations, engraved by W. Mason. Sydney.

„ —FRAGMENTS OF KAMILAROI GRAMMAR. By the Rev. W. Ridley, B.A.

„ —LINKS AND DIVERGENCIES OF THE AUSTRALIAN LANGUAGES AND TRIBES. By the Rev. W. Ridley, B.A.

Mr. Ridley is an accomplished Presbyterian clergyman, who for some years travelled in the interior of this Colony, zealously endeavouring to spread the light of Christianity among the native tribes. The fragmentary works above mentioned are the results of his studies of the aboriginal language. It is much to be regretted that the author did not proceed further in his researches. The origin of the various tribes inhabiting Australia, and of their dialects, are questions which still remain to be settled.

In this, as in other instances, it is to the labours of the Missionaries that the learned world is indebted for what little knowledge it possesses on the subject. More, perhaps, might have been done on this subject than has been done among us.

With the exception of the works mentioned here, and of a chapter in Dr. Lang's work on Cooksland, there is no contribution of much importance from any Australian writer. In speaking of our aboriginals, Mr. Ridley says,—

" Whatever may be the future that awaits them, I think the ascertained symmetry and exactitude of their languages, and the tenacity with which they hold their peculiar customs, clearly indicate—what monuments of stone and brass record of other nations—that they have been in past ages comparatively an intelligent people."

Some important remarks on this subject will be found in a lecture on the " Aborigines of Australia," delivered by Mr. Ridley, in September, 1864, and subsequently published :—

" The languages of the Australians," he says, " are multitudinous and elaborate. As the rapidly advancing science of Philology enlarges its survey, the Australian tongues will be found to furnish matter worthy of the study of the profoundest philologists. I shall attempt no more at present than to state a few facts illustrative of the peculiarities of this family of languages. Within the comparatively small circuit of my journeys in the interior, I met with twenty-five different languages. Though they are linked by resemblances which clearly prove them to be all derived from one source, they are so diverse in their vocabularies that they cannot be called dialects merely. The differences between them are not like those between the dialects of Attica and Laconia, or between those of Yorkshire and Middlesex—shades of pronunciation, with a few peculiar local words. On the contrary, the words in which identity can be traced, in two or more Australian languages, are the exceptions, not the rule. Some languages are limited to an area of some thirty or fifty miles square. A few seem to have a much wider use. The following are the names of some languages spoken in the interior.—(1.) Kamilaroi ; (2.) Wolaroi ; (3.) Wiraiaroi ; (4.) Wailwun ; (5.) Kogai ; (6.) Pikumbul ; (7.) Paiamba ; (8.) Kingki. The first five of these are named after their *negatives*. In the first, ' Kamil' signifies ' no'; in the second, ' Wol' is ' no'; in the third, ' Wira' is ' no'; in the fourth, ' Wail' is ' no'; in the fifth, ' Ko' is ' no.' In Pikumbul, on the other hand, ' piku' means ' yes'; so that the Australian aborigines, in this instance, named their language on the same principle on which the French acted in distinguishing the dialects of France, as ' Langue d'Oc' and ' Langue d'Oyl.'

" While the vocables differ widely, the grammatical structure of these languages marks their unity most fully. They are all characterized, like the German, by great facility in forming derivatives and compounds. Nouns, adjectives, and pronouns, are turned into verbs by means of affixes. The most remarkable feature in Australian languages is common to them all; it is the elastic power of modification in the verbs. Going eastward from Britain, we find this feature in language constantly increasing. The Greek has a middle voice in addition to the active and passive. The Hebrew has also intensive, causative, and reflective voices. The Australian languages have, besides these, permissive and reciprocal voices. The Rev. L. E. Threlkeld has enumerated no less than *fifteen* modifications or voices of the verb. In the tenses, one inflection signifies a little past—another refers to yesterday—another to a distant past—so of the future. The aborigines are very exact in the use of their numerous inflections. And the marvellous flexibility and precision of their language constitute the second notable relic of antiquity which they have preserved amid their decay. A language capable of expressing, by inflection, minute shades of thought, must have been the channel of communication between minds endowed with considerable acumen and power of generalization."

1857.—A FRENCH GRAMMAR, *with Conversazione Exercises.* By P. A. Dutruc, author of *L'Echo de la bonne Societe, &c., &c.* London and Sydney.

1857.—LITERARY RECREATIONS IN FRENCH AND ENGLISH, *including the Parterre of Flora.* By P. A. Dutrue. London.

The author of these works has been engaged for many years past in the tuition of his native language. He is now Reader in the French Language and Literature to the University of Sydney. The works are carefully compiled, and are in general use among students.

1866.—KAMILAROI, DIPPIL, AND TURRUBUL : *Languages Spoken by the Australian Aborigines.* By the Rev. Wm. Ridley, M.A., of the University of Sydney, Minister of the Presbyterian Church of New South Wales.

Mr. Ridley has embodied in this work the full result of his philological inquiries. It has been prepared for the Exhibition.

ETHNOLOGY.

1834.—VIEW OF THE ORIGIN AND MIGRATIONS OF THE POLY-
NESIAN NATION; *demonstrating their ancient Discovery and
progressive Settlement of the Continent of America.* By John
Dunmore Lang, D.D., Senior Minister of the Scots Church,
and Principal of the Australian College, Sydney ; Author of
" An Historical and Statistical Account of New South
Wales." London. 8vo., 256 pages.

It would not be too much to say that this is one of the most
valuable ethnological treatises ever written. In pursuing his
inquiries into the origin of the Polynesiaus, the author stumbled,
as it were, on one of the most ingenious solutions of a difficult
problem that philosophy has achieved. The work cannot be read
without forming a high opinion of the author's capacity for
philosophic investigation. It is well known that all his writings,
numerous as they are, have been produced under circumstances
by no means favourable to literary compositiou. " It would have
given me much pleasure to have had it in my power to spend a
few days in the library of the British Museum, to collect facts and
illustrations bearing on the subject of investigation in the
following pages, from works that are not elsewhere obtainable.
But, unfortunately, the only time I have been able to devote to
literary labour for several years past, has been the time I have
passed on ship-board, either amid storms and icebergs in the
high latitudes of the southern hemisphere, or beneath vertical
suns within the tropics ; where the only books to be had, in
addition to the few odd volumes in oue's own trunk, are the stars
of heaven by night, and the flying fish and dolphin by day." A
work devoted to such a subject as the origin of the Polynesian
Nations would peculiarly require the assistance of a library ; and

ships' cabins are about as propitious to literary labour as the cells of a gaol. But the "View" does not seem to have suffered materially from the disadvantages under which it was produced.

Dr. Lang first proceeds to prove that the inhabitants of the South Sea Islands are of Asiatic origin. The proofs advanced are directed to similarity of character, customs, and languages :— (1) Distinction of castes ; (2) Institution of *Taboo ;* (3) Rite of Circumcision ; (4) Resemblance of Idols ; (5) Resemblance in physical conformation and general character between the South Sea Islander and the Malay—prevalence of Asiatic customs in the South Sea Islands—of modes of thinking and peculiarities of action ; (7) Tradition among the Islanders that their forefathers came from the north-west ; (8) Similarity of clothing in Sumatra and the Islands—the East India practice of chewing *betel*, prevalent in the Duke of York's Island ; (9) Identity of language among the islanders, and striking resemblance between their language and that used in the Indian Archipelago. "The South Sea Islanders and the various tribes of Malays inhabiting the islands of the Indian Archipelago are of kindred origin ; and the languages of all these islanders are merely dialects of the same ancient and primitive tongue." Here follow some acute remarks with regard to these dialects, and the errors of distinguished writers on the subject. Dr. Lang then proceeds to point out some striking resemblances between the languages of China and Polynesia, from which he concludes that "both the nations and the languages of China and Polynesia have sprung from the same ancient and prolific source ; and that the line of demarcation which Professor Blumenbach has attempted to draw between the Mongolian and Malayan races of mankind is purely imaginary."

Having thus demonstrated, as he conceives, the identity of origin of the South Sea Islanders and the Malays of the Indian Archipelago, and referred this origin to the continent of Asia—

Dr. Lang then proceeds to the second step in his argument, which is to shew " in what manner islands so remote from each other could have been successfully peopled by a nation so comparatively low in the scale of civilization as the Polynesians." The first argument advanced on this point is historical. The author recalls the later days of the Malayan Empire in the East, when it was first known to Europeans, and when they possessed more than one flourishing and powerful kingdom. He relates many incidents of their national existence at that period, for the purpose of illustrating their power on the sea. He glances at the probability of the Indian Archipelago having been " traversed from time immemorial both by the Chinese and the Malays," and at the commercial intercourse of the former with the Moluccas, long before those islands were seized by Europeans, and of the latter with the north coast of New Holland. From these facts, he concludes that maritime adventure was a characteristic of their race, and that from the earliest times they have been addicted to voyaging in search of new lands. In this manner, the islands of the South Sea, one after another, received their first inhabitants. An additional argument is found in the practice among the islanders, after the conclusion of a civil war, of exterminating the vanquished party, either by putting them to death on shore, or by forcing them to take to their canoes.

At this stage of his argument, Dr. Lang takes up another question—the origin of cannibalism. His theory on this point is not the least ingenious portion of his work. He ascribes it to the necessity under which the savages were placed, while floating about at sea in their canoes, wholly unprovided with food, and with no means of procuring it. Such a necessity has been experienced by Europeans. And he supposes that, when the canoes at last touched the shores of some new island, the practice was continued, and became a national habit.

Dr. Lang next adverts to "the grand objection" usually urged against the Asiatic origin of the islanders. This is " the supposed uniform prevalence of the north-east and south-east trade winds within the tropics;" but the testimony of La Perouse and other navigators is decisively opposed to this idea. He then refers to the arguments of De Zuniga, a Spanish author, who ridicules the supposition of an Asiatic origin; and asserts that " the Indians of the Phillipine Islands are descended from the aborigines of Chili and Peru"—that is, that the islanders came originally from America. This theory of the Spanish author led Dr. Lang considerably further in his voyage of discovery than he at first proposed; but the result of his researches constitutes the gist of his volume. His argument he states in these words :—" There is abundant reason to believe that America was originally peopled from the continent of Asia; not, as is generally supposed, by way of the Aleutian Islands, at the entrance of Behring's Straits, but by way of the South Sea Islands, and across the widest part of the Pacific Ocean."

To the establishment of this proposition the remainder of the work is devoted. Identity of customs and of language, as before, forms the main support of the Doctor's theory. So much research is brought to bear upon the question, that it is doubtful whether the book would have displayed more learning had it been concocted and written in the British Museum, instead of a cabin at sea. It is difficult to resist the conclusion that the author has satisfactorily established his theory. From beginning to end, his arguments present one unbroken chain. Ethnological problems are seldom susceptible of decisive proof one way or the other; but there are probably few works of the kind which may be read with more satisfaction than this of Dr. Lang.

A notice of this work appeared in the Journal of the Royal Geographical Society. Lengthy extracts from its pages were given, and the writer expressed a favourable opinion of the theory advanced with regard to the American Aborigines. " We think that he has established his main point, and, moreover, that he has brought within a moderate compass a great many curious facts and coincidences." In the Encyclopædia Britannica, art. "America," the theory advanced by Dr. Lang is propounded as a reasonable view of the matter. No reference, however, is made to his volume. This is enough to shew that the theory itself has met with general acceptance.

The "View" was largely noticed in various American periodicals. The " *Princeton Review*" of 1841 contained an article on it, in the course of which the writer discussed the theories of various writers relating to the Aborigines. " Dr. Lang's book," he says, " is here introduced, because this learned and enterprising clergyman has brought forward a new theory." The Reviewer agreed with Dr. Lang as to the Asiatic extraction of the Polynesians, but not as to the Polynesian extraction of the American Indians. He maintained that America was originally peopled by " colonies from many different nations and countries," and that Dr. Lang was at fault in his notions respecting the languages of the natives. " Dr. Lang seems to take it for granted that all the American languages have diverged from one point, and are but dialects of the same original tongue, but this is nohow consonant with the observed facts of the case. Another error into which he has been led by his hypothesis is, that the language of Asia having been originally monosyllabic. the American languages were at first of this structure also. Nothing can be more remote from the truth." The *American Quarterly Review* of 1836 also weighed the arguments advanced by Dr. Lang. With respect to the Polynesians, it said : " The hypothesis of their Asiatic origin is maintained with great confidence by Dr. Lang, and he has given a very good summary of the arguments in support of it." It then quoted his arguments, but expressed no opinion on the theory itself. With reference to the alleged identity of language among the Americans and the Islanders, it considered that no case was made out, inasmuch as the American dialects were not monosyllabic, as stated by Dr. Lang.

The " View" is quoted in a very learned work entitled *Crania Americana*, by Dr. Morton, an American author. It was also made use of in a different fashion by another writer. Mr. Williams, generally known as the Martyr of Erromanga, published an account of his travels, in conjunction with Mr. Ellis, the author of the *Polynesian Researches*. In this publication, he propounded the American theory started by Dr. Lang, and supported it with the Doctor's arguments. The contents of the " View" were cleverly squeezed into ten or twelve pages, without the slightest reference to the author.

PHYSICAL SCIENCE.

1834.—WANDERINGS IN NEW SOUTH WALES, BATAVIA, PEDIR COAST, SINGAPORE, AND CHINA; *being the Journal of a Naturalist in those Countries, during* 1832-3-4. By George Bennett, Esq., F.L.S., F.R.C.S., &c. London. 2 vols., 8vo.

The *Quarterly Review* devoted an article to the consideration of this work, and commended it highly. It began :

" If our readers are as weary of new novels as we confess ourselves to be, they will thank us for pointing out a book of travels which carries one rapidly and pleasantly over a wide diversity of sea and land ; presents many objects of natural history and traits of social peculiarity well calulated to excite and gratify our curiosity ; and is distinguished by a merit now exceedingly rare among writers of this once rough-spun class, namely, freedom from the cant and slang of sentiment. Mr. Bennett sometimes, no doubt, treats of serious subjects in too light a vein ; but we acknowledge that, as his offences in this way are not numerous, we are willing to overlook them on account of the satisfaction which results from the absence of pseudo-poetical raptures about nothing. We do not pretend to class Mr. Bennett, on the whole, with such authors as Capt. Basil Hall and Sir Francis Head ; but he has, in common with them, what must be felt as among their chief excellencies—a manly temperament, and a thorough scorn of puerile rhetoric."

1837.—A CATALOGUE OF THE SPECIMENS OF NATURAL HISTORY AND MISCELLANEOUS CURIOSITIES *deposited in the Australian Museum.* Sydney. 71 pages.

1851.—HISTORY AND DESCRIPTION OF THE SKELETON OF A NEW SPERM WHALE, *lately set up in the Australian Museum*, by W. S. Wall, Curator; *together with some account of a new genus of Sperm Whale, called Euphysetes.* Two plates. Sydney. 8vo., 66 pages.

1860.—Researches in the Southern Gold Fields of New South Wales. By The Rev. W. B. Clarke, M.A., F.G S., F.R.G.S., M.Z.S. Member of the Geological Society of France, Correspondent of the Imperial-Royal Geological State Institute of Austria, Hon. Member of the New Zealand Society, of the Royal Society of Tasmania, &c., &c., &c. Sydney. 8vo., 385 pages.

The author states that this work was hastily composed, in compliance with the wishes of persons who were anxious to supply intending gold diggers with reliable information. There existed at the time a strong belief that gold abounded in the Alpine regions of the Colony, at Kiandra and other localities, and "a rush" was the natural result. That gold existed in that part of the country was first pointed out by the author, in his Reports to the Government. They are reprinted in the ' Researches.'

In an Appendix to this work, Mr. Clarke has collected and arranged the various facts connected with the great discovery of gold. The question raised by Mr. Davison, in the work already noticed, is largely illustrated by them. With reference to Mr. Hargraves and his book, Mr. Clarke says :—

" He has given some particulars of his early history in the prefatory observations to a book entitled, ' Australia and its Gold Fields,' understood to have been in part the work of a gentleman now living in the Colony, and who had delivered at public lectures the substance, if not the *ipsissima verba*, of the two first chapters. As the end of the book contains three letters, containing ' A new Theory of Gold, by Simpson Davison, Esq.,' the middle of the work is all that, I presume, strictly belongs to the author ; and I wish it did not, as it contains at least one thing not true (viz., that I ever purchased gold of any one), and was written so as to serve the purpose of the author, at the expense of my reputation.

" If this book had been printed in the Colony, where his pretensions could be sifted, and not in London, where he became a detractor of those who, being 13,000 miles away, could not answer him on the spot,—neither would Sir

Roderick Murchison have quoted it as confirming his own views respecting the Ural, nor would the Editor of the Year Book have ventured to state that anything said in Mr. Hargraves' book could refute my own assertions.

" During his stay in California, Mr. Hargrave says, he became convinced of the similarity of California and Australia, and expressed his persuasion to his friend Davison, that ' we should soon hear of a discovery of gold in the latter country ; and his determination, if not discovered before his return to New South Wales, to prosecute a systematic search for it.' This certainly was well enough for a man who ' did not like prospecting,' and is quite contradicted by Mr. Davison's statement, as well as by letters from Mr. Rudder. He came back to this Colony in 1851, to look after his family affairs and ' domestic ties' as Mr. Davison says ; but, according to himself, for the purpose of making the discovery of gold.

" Well, what did he shew ? What did he, according to his own testimony, procure from the spot in which he says he felt as if he was ' surrounded by gold?' Did he get a pennyweight ? He got ' five little particles' that ' did not amount to a grain in weight,' and which the Colonial Secretary said were so ' very minute,' that ' they were scarcely visible.'

" No wonder Mr. Hargraves felt disheartened, and contemplated his return to California. But the Fates were propitious. Having taught his guides (Tom and Lister) to use the cradle, *they* rocked him into celebrity. The four ounces which *they* found enabled him to make his claim upon the Government.

" Honours and offerings, public dinners, and complimentary tea services, now flocked in upon the 'first discoverer,' who rose to affluence upon the result of Messrs. Tom and Lister's prospecting, which they had been trying for a year and more in the same place, on a less profitable plan.

" Has Mr. Hargraves no merit ? Certainly. Very great merit is due to him for teaching his guides to wash the earth after the Californian fashion."

The author of these " Researches," is one of the most distinguished geologists of the day. The following biographical items concerning him are taken from an article published in the *Herald* some years ago :—

" Mr. Clarke commenced the study of geology as early as the year 1817, under Dr. E. D. Clarke, the great traveller, and Professor Sedgwick. This was not a mere study of books, but a personal examination of the most celebrated formations in Europe. He travelled extensively in England and Wales, and on the Continent, from 1820 to 1839, not omitting a single year. In 1820, he visited the Lake District of Westmoreland and Cumberland, and the Isle of Man; in 1821, the Coal Fields of Staffordshire and Derbyshire; in 1822, the Lake District and North Wales; in 1823, the chalk and oolitic and tertiary districts of Yorkshire and Lincolnshire; in 1824, the chalk districts of Sussex and Normandy; in 1825, the central and southern parts of France, the Alps, and the north of Italy; in 1826, the Netherlands; in 1827, the Netherlands, the Rhenish Provinces, Prussia, and Holland; in 1828, Belgium and Ardennes, and the tertiary districts of Nassau; in 1829, the volcanic districts of the Rhine and Moselle, completing also a survey of the counties of Suffolk, Norfolk, and Essex, commenced in 1827; in 1830, the chalk districts and older formations of the frontiers of France and Belgium; in 1831, Dorsetshire and the west of England; in 1832, Dorsetshire and the Isle of Wight, Sussex, and the south-west of England; in 1833, the coal beds, &c., of the Boulounais; in 1835, the north of France; in 1836, the Channel Islands and the Isle of Portland; in 1837, the new red sandstone districts of Staffordshire, Cheshire, and Lancashire; in 1838, the Silurian old red sandstone and coal districts of Shropshire, Herefordshire, Monmouthshire, and South Wales; and in 1837, the Colony of the Cape of Good Hope. Besides these regular explorations, other journeys were taken to interesting localities.   *   *   *   *   *   *

" It has not been merely in the acquisition of knowledge that Mr. Clarke has distinguished himself. Before his arrival in this Colony, his labours were known and recognized. In D'Archiac's " History of the Progress of Geology," honourable mention is made of his contributions on geology; and for a succession of years, papers from his pen appeared in scientific works, the enumeration of which would require a catalogue combining almost all the topics within the range of geological inquiry. Many of them are found in the *Magazine of Natural History*, and in the *Transactions and Proceedings of the Geological Society.*

" Since his arrival in this Colony, Mr. Clarke has been most laborious in his contributions, which are now circulated through the scientific world. His Reports to the Government of New South Wales have been revised and abstracted by M. Delesse, in his tract *Sur le Gisement et sur l'Exploitation de l'Or en Australie.* The respectable publication issued by the Royal Society of Tasmania was enriched with many papers contributed by Mr. Clarke; and it is to be regretted that they are not published in a more convenient form, relating, as they chiefly do, to the geological phenomena of this country."

The sum of £1,000 was voted to Mr. Clarke by the Government of New South Wales, and a similar sum was voted by the Victorian Legislature. The Government of Tasmania offered him the appointment of Geological Surveyor, with a salary of £600 per annum. This offer he declined.

1860.—GATHERINGS OF A NATURALIST IN AUSTRALIA : *being Observations principally on the Animal and Vegetable Productions of New South Wales, New Zealand, and some of the Austral Islands.* By George Bennett, M.D., F.L.S., F.Z.S.; Fellow of the Royal College of Surgeons of England; Member of the Medical Faculty of the University of Sydney, New South Wales; and Author of " Wanderings in New South Wales, Singapore, and China." London. 8vo., 456 pages.

The following criticisms on this work will suffice to give a correct idea of its character and value.

The *British Quarterly Review* said:

" This is just such a volume as a reader with a taste for Natural History will open with pleasure, and close with regret. It has sufficient specialty about it to fix the attention of the ablest labourers in this department of knowledge, for it conveys a vast amount of original information respecting the *Fauna* and *Flora* of the Austral regions. But to those who have been accustomed to look upon Australia as a land whose animals were stupid marsupials, whose forests were mere scrub, whose trees were too tame to produce timber, and whose indigenous men were only a riper species of ape, this work will be the pleasant unsealing of a once popular delusion. Amongst other vegetable and animal curiosities, Dr. Bennett will introduce them to the gigantic stinging nettle of New South Wales, which frequently reach a height of fifty feet (with a circumference of twenty), and sometimes have been known to attain an elevation of more than one hundred and twenty. The leaves are from a foot to a foot and a half in breadth, and the powers of the vegetable are such that horses are disabled for days if the poisonous fluid finds its way into their veins. The reader will be told of fish-bone trees, rice-paper plants, giant lilies, Christmas-trees, gum-trees from whose leaves it has been proposed to manufacture gas; and, in the animal kingdom, he will hear with interest of glass eels, which are so transparent that you may read through them; luminous sharks, flying foxes, colossal cranes, and rare moruks or cassowaries; but more especially he will learn all about that famous living paradox, the ornithorynchus or water-mole, to which the author devotes an entire chapter. Dr. Bennett carries his enthusiasm as a naturalist to a gallant extreme. He is the man to take a gymnotus by the hand, to tests its electrical powers, or allow himself to be bitten by a tarantula, to ascertain whether its bite is curable by musical strains. Having heard much respecting the venomous properties of the spur of the water-mole, he made it a point to experiment upon the first specimen he captured; but though he gave the anomalous quadruped every opportunity for wounding him, and indeed, insisted upon receiving a few scratches, no evil consequence resulted; and thus the character of the creature was relieved from an unfounded aspersion."

The *Westminster Review* spoke of it in the following terms :—

" Although many of Dr. Bennett's ' Gatherings' have already been presented to the public through various channels, yet we heartily welcome their appearance in a collective form, with the additional materials which he has now, for the first time, brought forth from his budget of ' Australasian Zoology and Botany,' altogether constituting a handsome and beautifully illustrated volume. To Dr. Bennett we are indebted for our first knowledge of the animal of the pearly nautilus, the type of those chambered cephalopods that have ranged through nearly the whole series of geological periods; and it is somewhat aggravating now to learn that living nautili are so plentiful at the Fiji Islands, that they are caught for food in wicker traps baited like lobster-pots, and are eaten *curried* by the natives. Dr. Bennett was also the discoverer of the new and remarkable species of cassowary found only in New Britain, and known by its native name of mooruk; and to him also we are indebted for most of our knowledge of the physiology and habits of the anomalous ornithorynchus, as of its congener the echidna, and also of the remarkable jabrin or gigantic crane. Our Zoological Gardens have largely profited by the zeal with which he has purveyed for them among the

curiosities supplied by his adopted country ; and he has also done much to
direct attention to the practical value of many forms of its vegetation, which
might otherwise have been disregarded. We trust that on his return thither,
he will long continue to render those valuable services to science for which
his antipodean residence has afforded the opportunity, but which has mainly
sprung from an earnestness which would make an opportunity for itself in
any locality, however familiar."

1863.—THE TRANSACTIONS OF THE ENTOMOLOGICAL SOCIETY OF NEW SOUTH WALES. Part I.

The first monthly meeting of this Society was held on the
5th May, 1862. It consisted of twenty-eight members, but this
number has since increased. At the Annual General Meeting,
held on the 30th January, 1863, the President, Mr. William
Macleay, read an Address, from which I take the following ;—

" The advantages which the original promoters of the Institution anticipated were of a two-fold character. They wished to give all who were
interested in the science of Entomology, opportunities of social intercourse ;
and they also wished to be the means of assisting in the publication of such
papers connected with the science as might be deemed worthy of their
sanction.

" Viewing these as the main objects of the Society, I think I am justified
in saying that it has already been as successful as its most sanguine promoters could have desired. A number of gentlemen, previously unknown to
each other, have been afforded opportunities of meeting together, which,
without the intervention of the Society, would perhaps never have existed ;
an impetus has been given to collecting, in a degree hitherto unknown in the
Colony ; and from the facilities given of communicating information, an
unusual amount of observation has been concentrated in the history and
habits of the insect tribes."

The Entomological Society numbered among its members
one of the most distinguished naturalists of the present day.
This was Mr. William Sharp Macleay. He was the eldest son of
the late Alexander Macleay, F.R.S. and F.L.S., formerly Colonial
Secretary of the Colony. He was born in London, in 1792, and
arrived here in 1839. Previous to his residence among us, he

held various important offices in the service of the Imperial Government. Several years of his life were spent in Paris, where he became a personal friend of Cuvier and other men of science. He resided in this Colony from the time of his arrival till his death in 1865. During this period, he distinguished himself by his devotion to scientific pursuits, and by various efforts to promote the cultivation of science in the Colony. He was considered, during his lifetime, 'the first of living entomologists.' His collection of insects, especially of those peculiar to this country, was the most extensive and most valuable in existence. His mind, however, did not confine itself to one department of science. Botany, zoology, and geology, were favourite pursuits. A list of papers contributed by him to different scientific journals in England forms an ample testimony to the range and depth of his attainments.

The Transactions of the Entomological Society are handsomely printed and illustrated, and contain accounts of the various specimens exhibited, and papers read, at the monthly meetings. From them it is obvious that the foundation of the Society has proved of much use in furthering the interests of science in our community. Comparatively little would have been achieved in the department of entomology but for its existence. The efforts of individuals not connected by any common tie seldom prove of much importance, in a young community. There is little stimulus to exertion in research, and still less to the publication of papers. In the latter respect, the existence of this Society is especially useful.

1864.—CATALOGUE OF AUSTRALIAN LAND SHELLS. By James C. Cox, M.D., F.R.C.S., Edinburgh. Sydney. 44 pages.

The principal object of the Catalogue is, as stated by Dr. Cox, "to give a complete list of all the Genera and Species of Australian Land Shells known to be described, together with descriptions of such new species as have not hitherto been recorded in the principal Australian collections,—and to record correct localities."

Dr. Cox is one of the most zealous cultivators of science in the Colony. He is a member of the Philosophical and Entomological Societies, and has read many papers on various scientific subjects. His researches are principally devoted to Conchology.

1864.—AUSTRALIAN LEPIDOPTERA AND THEIR TRANSFORMATIONS. By A. W. Scott, M.A., Ash Island, Hunter River, New South Wales. London. Parts I, II, III.

An important contribution to the general sum of scientific knowledge. The author has devoted himself for many years past to the study of local entomology, and the volume cited contains the results of his researches. It is magnificently illustrated by drawings from the pencils of his daughters—drawings which could hardly be surpassed in point of accuracy and finish. The publication was an expensive one, but twenty-five copies only were disposed of in the Colony.

1864.—CATALOGUE OF MAMMALIA IN THE COLLECTION OF THE AUSTRALIAN MUSEUM. By Gerard Krefft, Curator and Secretary. Sydney. 8vo. 136 pages.

1865.—TWO PAPERS ON THE VERTEBRATA OF THE LOWER MURRAY AND DARLING, AND OF THE SNAKES OF SYDNEY : *read before the Philosophical Society of New South Wales, 10th September*, 1862. By Gerard Krefft. Sydney. 8vo. 60 pages.

Mr. Krefft was born and educated in Brunswick. After a visit to America, he spent some time in this country, having been attracted by the newly discovered gold mines. The Government of Victoria employed him to visit the districts of the Lower Murray and Darling, and subsequently conferred upon him an appointment in the National Museum in Melbourne. This he soon after resigned, in order to return to Europe. During his stay in Europe he visited the principal Museums, and, on his return to Australia, the Trustees of the Australian Museum in this Colony appointed him Assistant Curator, and shortly afterwards, Acting Curator and Secretary. Mr. Krefft is a member of various Scientific Societies in England and Germany, and, in this Colony, of the Entomological and Philosophical Societies. Few men can exceed him in zeal, and as a practical observer his services to this country are of very great value.

1866.—THE TRANSACTIONS OF THE PHILOSOPHICAL SOCIETY OF NEW SOUTH WALES. Vol. 1. Sydney. 8vo., 374 pages.

A Society was established in Sydney, under this title, many years ago, but it speedily died out. Some of the papers read at its meetings were published by the well-known Barron Field, in 1825. The present Society was established at the instance of Sir W. Denison, in 1856. He was then Governor of the Colony, and was deeply interested in scientific investigations. The Society numbers about 200 members, and papers of considerable value may be found among its transactions.

GEOGRAPHY.

1845.—AUSTRALIA, FROM PORT MACQUARIE TO MORETON BAY, with descriptions of the Natives, their manners and customs; the geology, natural productions, fertility, and resources of that region; first explored and surveyed by order of the Colonial Government. By Clement Hodgkinson. London. 8vo.

The author was an officer in the Survey Department of this Colony.

1848.—A GEOGRAPHICAL DICTIONARY, OR GAZETTEER OF THE AUSTRALIAN COLONIES; *their Physical and Political Geography, together with a Brief Notice of all the Capitals, Principal Towns, and Villages; also of Rivers, Bays, Gulfs, Mountains, Population, and General Statistics.* Illustrated with numerous Maps and Drawings. By W. H. Wells, Surveyor. Sydney, 8vo., 438 pages.

1851.—THE AUSTRALIAN GEOGRAPHY, WITH THE SHORES OF THE PACIFIC AND THOSE OF THE INDIAN OCEAN. By Lieut.-Col. Sir T. L. Mitchell, Surveyor General of Sydney, author of *Tropical Australia,* &c, *To which is added, an Appendix, containing a correct Account of the recent Gold Discovery in that Continent.* Sydney. 8vo.

1863.—THE GEOGRAPHY OF NEW SOUTH WALES, PHYSICAL, INDUSTRIAL, AND POLITICAL. By W. Wilkins, Chief Inspector of National Schools, Sydney. Sydney. 12mo.

1866.—BAILLIERE'S NEW SOUTH WALES GAZETTEER AND ROAD GUIDE, *containing the most recent and accurate Information as to every Place in the Colony.* Compiled by R. P. Whitworth. With Map. Sydney. 8vo., 664 pages.

LAW.

1835.—The Australian Magistrate : *or, a Guide to the duties of a Justice of the Peace for the Colony of New South Wales. Also, a brief Summary of the Law of Landlord and Tenant.* By J. H. Plunkett, A.B., *Her Majesty's Solicitor General of New South Wales.* Sydney. 8vo.

This work is now in its second edition, the last, by Mr. Wilkinson, of the Colonial Bar, having recently appeared. Its contents embrace the whole of those legal details which occupy the attention of our magistrates, and are arranged with great clearness and conciseness. It is now a standard work, and its extreme usefulness has recommended it to the legal profession and the magistracy in the neighbouring Colonies, as well as in New South Wales. The editor, Mr. Wilkinson, has been engaged for many years past in reporting the common law cases decided in the Supreme Court of the Colony.

1842.—The Insolvent Law of New South Wales, *with practical directions and forms.* By W. W. Burton, Esq., one of the Judges of the Supreme Court of that Colony. Sydney.

1843.—The Constitution, Rules, and Practice of the Supreme Court of New South Wales. By Alfred Stephen, Esq., one of the Judges of that Court. Sydney.

1844.—Acts and Ordinances of the Governor and Council of New South Wales, and Acts of Parliament enacted for and applied to the Colony, *with Notes and Index.* By Thomas Callaghan, Esq., Barrister-at-Law. Sydney. 3 vols., 8vo.

A useful compilation. The author was subsequently appointed a District Court Judge, aud died a few years ago.

1846.—Reserved and Equity Judgments of the Supreme Court of New South Wales, *delivered during the year* 1845. Sydney.

1851.—Supplement to the Supreme Court Practice, *with Acts of Council, and Notes of Cases (chiefly on points of practice)*. By M. Henry Stephen, Esq., Barrister-at-law. Sydney.

1856.—Supreme Court Practice. *The Rules of Court and Enactments affecting actions and other proceedings at Law.* Sydney.

This compilation was the work of His Honor Sir Alfred Stephen, Chief Justice of the Colony. It is of much practical value to the legal profession.

1858.—Lecture on Law, *delivered at the Mechanics' School of Arts, Pitt-street, Sydney, August 3rd,* 1858. By J. F. Hargrave, Esq., M.A., of Trinity College, Cambridge, and of Lincoln's Inn, and the Supreme Court of New South Wales ; Barrister-at-Law, Author of " A Treatise on the Thellusson Act," and Editor of the First Volume of the 21st English Edition of Blackstone's " Commentaries on the Laws of England." Sydney.

1859.—The District Courts Act of 1858, and The District Courts Act Amendment Act of 1859, *with practical Notes.* By W. J. Foster, Barrister-at-law. Sydney. 8vo.

Contains an introduction explaining the nature, jurisdiction, and proceedings of the District Courts of New South Wales, and the alterations effected in the Courts of General and Quarter Sessions, illustrated by numerous authorities ; and also an Appendix, containing the rules of practice and forms of proceedings, together with several useful Acts of the Colonial Legislature.

1860.—Introductory Lecture on General Jurisprudence, *delivered at the University of Sydney, March 5th,* 1860. By J. F. Hargrave, Esq., M.A., Barrister-at-Law, Reader in General Jurisprudence for the Years 1859-60, and Her Majesty's Attorney General for the Colony of New South Wales ; annexed to which is a " Syllabus of the two Courses of Lectures on General Jurisprudence," *delivered at the University of Sydney, during the Years* 1859-60-61. Sydney.

The learned author of these lectures is now a Puisne Judge of the Supreme Court.

1861.—A Collection of Statutes affecting New South Wales—*containing all the Statutes of practical utility to the present time.* Edited by Henry Cary, District Court Judge. Sydney. 2 vols., imperial 8vo.

A very useful compilation, comprising not only the Acts of the local Legislature, but those of the Imperial Parliament which have been adopted here. The Statutes are arranged in the order of subject, alphabetically. Mr. Cary is the son of the Rev. H. F. Cary, known to Literature as the translator of Dante. In 1846, Mr. Cary published the articles contributed by his father to the *London Magazine,* on the " Early French Poets," prefixing an introductory sketch of the History of French Poetry. He has not since made any contributions to Literature ; but his reputation as a classical scholar is considerable. The Acts of Parliament passed in this Colony are now printed and published at the Government Printing Office, at the close of each Session.

1861.—The Public General Statutes of New South Wales. Sydney. 4 vols.

1861.—The Private Acts of New South Wales. Sydney. 1 vol.

This is a collection of Acts of Parliament, comprising those of the local Legislature, and also those of the Imperial Parliament which have been adopted in the Colony. It is published by authority of the Government. The Statutes are published at the close of each Session.

1862.—Reports of Cases argued and determined in the Supreme Court of New South Wales. By W. H. Wilkinson, Esq., and W. Owen, Esq., Barristers-at-law. Sydney.

Four volumes of these Reports have already appeared.

1863.—The Supreme Court of New South Wales. *In Equity. Consolidated Standing Rules, made on 4th July, 1863, and which are to take effect after 30th September, 1863.* By authority. Sydney.

Index to the above. Compiled by Rees Rutland Jones, B.A.

1866.—The New South Wales Magisterial Digest : *a practical Guide for Magistrates, Clerks of Petty Sessions, Attorneys, Constables; and others, comprising indictable offences and summary convictions, with their punishments, penalties, procedure, &c., being alphabetically and tabularly arranged; together with other proceedings before Justices, adapted practically to the provisions of Sir John Jervis's Acts, with forms, cases, copies, notes, and observations.* By Henry Connell, junr., Clerk of Petty Sessions, Kiama. Sydney. 8vo., 886 pages.

This work is, to some extent, a similar one to that issued by Mr. Plunkett, already noticed ; but it is much more comprehensive. The tabular arrangement of offences, with the penalties attached to them, enables the reader to find information at a glance, which, iu any other form, could not be obtained without some labour. Every point likely to occur in practice in the lower Courts is fully commented on, and the requisite authorities arranged with great care. As a practical work, it must be of great value to the officials for whose use it was principally prepared, while the style of publication is fully equal to that of the London law booksellers.

N

THEOLOGY.

1835.—OBSERVATIONS ON THE USE AND ABUSE OF THE SACRED SCRIPTURES, as exhibited in the Discipline and Practice of the Protestant and Catholic Communions. By the Rev. W. B. Ullathorne, V.G. Sydney.

The author was the Roman Catholic Vicar-General of the Colony, and is now Bishop of Birmingham.

1836.—THE LANGUAGE OF THEOLOGY INTERPRETED, in a Series of Short and Easy Lectures. By E. M. C. Bowen, a Settler in New South Wales (formerly a Lieutenant in H.M. 39th Regiment). Sydney. 8vo., 318 pages.

At the end of this work appears the following announcement:—" To appear in a year or two, in case the author of this work should recover the expenses,—" Interpretations of Scriptures, tested by aid of Facts, Experiments and Observations."

The author apparently did *not* recover his expenses, inasmuch as no vestige of the work announced can be found.

1840.—RELIGION AND EDUCATION IN AMERICA. By J. D. Lang.

The circumstances which led to the production of this work are stated by the author in the last edition of his History, p. 494 : " Certain matters having rendered it necessary that I should proceed to England once more in the year 1839, I embraced the opportunity, during my stay in the northern hemisphere, of crossing over to the United States of America. For as I then foresaw that the question as to the propriety of having a religious establishment in the Colonies at all would very soon be the great question in the Australian Colonies, I wished to ascertain for myself individually, before taking any prominent part in the discussion of that question, whether Christianity could support itself in any country, as was alleged it did in America, without the support of the State. My introductions in the United States were of the first order, including eminent men of all ranks and professions, from the President downwards. I visited eleven of the States, from Salem, in Massachusetts, to Charleston, in South Carolina; and my own observation abundantly confirmed the testimony I received from all quarters, viz., that Christianity could unquestionably maintain itself in the world by its own native and inherent energies, and that it required no pecuniary support from the State. On my return to England, I embodied the result of my observations in a work entitled " Religion and Education in America," which was published in London in the year 1840, and which, I soon ascertained, gave prodigious offence, both in Scotland and in New South Wales; salutary truths of that kind being, at this comparatively early period, by no means universally palatable."

1842.—SERMONS PREACHED IN ST. ANDREW'S CHURCH, SYDNEY, NEW SOUTH WALES. By the Rev. John M'Garvie, D.D. Sydney. 8vo., 394 pages.

1844.—TEN LECTURES, WITH HISTORICAL NOTICES, ILLUSTRATIVE OF THE ANTI-SCRIPTURAL CHARACTER AND PERNICIOUS TENDENCY OF THE DOCTRINES OF PUSEYISM. By James Fullerton, LL.D., Minister of the Scots Church, Pitt-street, Sydney. Sydney, 8vo., 220 pages.

1848.—LECTURES ON PROPHECY AND THE KINGDOM OF CHRIST. *Delivered in the Scots Church, Macquarie-street, Sydney, from April 16th to June 18th*, 1848. By the Rev. Barzillai Quaife. Sydney, 8vo., 240 pages.

1857.—MORMONISM; *or the Doctrines of the self-styled Latter-day Saints, compared with itself and the Bible, and found wanting.* By John Davis. Sydney. 8vo., 85 pages.

MISCELLANEOUS.

1825.—A Treatise on the Culture of the Vine, and the Art of Making Wine ; *compiled from the works of Choptal and other French Writers, and from the notes of the Compiler, during a residence in some of the Wine Provinces of France.* By James Busby. Australia. 8vo., 270 pages.

The author states that, previous to his emigration to New South Wales, he entertained a conviction that the vine could be profitably cultivated in the Colony, and that he visited the Wine Provinces of France for the purpose of acquiring information on that subject. The Treatise contains the results of his inquiries ; but, as its title indicates, it is rather a compilation than an original work.

This, and subsequent works by the same author, were reviewed in the *New South Wales Magazine* for September, 1833. We are there informed that the Treatise " fell dead from the press"; the failure being ascribed to the unsuitability of the work to the practical requirements of the colonists. It was a compilation adapted to those only who had already acquired some practical acquaintance with the mysteries of wine-making. At the time of its publication in Sydney, " few persons had thought of the vine as anything better than an ornament to their gardens, or an addition to their dessert."

This was the first book printed and published in the Colony. Mr. Busby was subsequently appointed " British Resident in New Zealand."

1826.—An Account of the state of Agriculture and Grazing in New South Wales. By James Atkinson. London.

The author was a Clerk in the Office of the Colonial Secretary in this Colony.

1829.—A Letter from Sydney, the principal Town of
Australasia. Edited by Robert Gouger. Together with
the outline of a System of Colonization. London. 8vo.,
222 pages.

A very lively though prejudiced account of society in Sydney,
as the author viewed it in 1829, will be found in his work.
Curiously enough, while he indulges in unsparing ridicule of
the colonists generally, he draws a glowing picture of the beauty
of the native-born women, and of the physical and mental
excellence of the native-born men. " The latitude of Sydney
corresponds exactly with that of Paphos ; and it is no less true
that the native Australians bear a stronger resemblance to the
modern Greeks than to any other people."

This work is criticised at some length in Sidney's " Australian
Colonies," and the authorship attributed to Edward Gibbon
Wakefield. "All that we know of Robert Gouger is, that he
was a Dissenter, of republican opinions, who served some time
in the French National Guard during the Revolution of July,
1830. He afterwards became Secretary of the South Australian
Society, and eventually Colonial Secretary in South Australia."
Sidney says that " a great sensation was produced in the literary
and political world" on the appearance of the " Letter from
Sydney," and that " it was soon known to be the production of
Wakefield." There are some remarkably fine passages in this
production ; and as it is now out of print and forgotten, the
quotation of one of them may be excused :—

" You remember that Genoese girl, before whom you trembled and I
became faint, though she only handed us some grapes. Do you remember
that, having recovered ourselves, we measured her eyelashes? Do you
remember how long they were, and how she laughed? Do you remember
that bright laugh, and how I patted her cheek, and told her that it was softer

than her country's velvet?   And how she blushed!—do you remember that?—
to the tips of her fingers and the roots of her hair?   And then how—do you
remember how—peasant as she was, and but just fifteen, she tossed her head
and stamped her little foot with the air of a queen?   And then how, on a
sudden, her large eyes were filled with tears; and the grace with which she
folded her arms across that charming bosom; and the tone—I hear it now—
the deep, grave, penetrating tone in which, half angry, half afraid, she at
once threatened us with her " Berto," and implored our respect?   We did
not care much for Mr. Berto, certainly; but did we not swear, both together,
that not a hair of her head should we hurt?   And when, flattered by our
involuntary devotion, she departed with a healthy lively step, shewing her
small, smooth ancles, and now and then turning her profile to us, and laughing
as before—did we not, dashing blades as we thought ourselves, snuffle and
blow our noses, and shake hands without the least motive, like two fools?
And afterwards, notwithstanding that gratuitous fit of friendship, did we not
feel jealous of each other for three days, though neither of us could hope
to see the little angel again?   Yes, you remember it all.   Well, just such
another girl as that brings fruit to my door every morning.

"I do not pretend, however, that *all* the girls of Australia are equally
beautiful; but I do declare what you know to be true of the Ligarian girls,—
that three out of four of them would be considered beauties in May Fair.
The cause—what is the cause?   As you have a reason for everything, I will
state my own notion on the subject.

"It was after you left me in Italy that I passed a miserable winter at
Turin, amongst one of the ugliest races of women in the world.   In March,
whilst the plain of the Po was still covered with deep frozen snow, and all
things above the snow were enveloped in dense, chilling, choking fog, I
removed to Genoa.   The old track over the Bochetta, by Gavi, was then the
only road across that part of the Apennines; and that track led over the
narrow top of the highest ridge, so that three turns of a wheel carried the
traveller from the climate of the Baltic, as it were, to that of the Mediterranean.   The contrast was most delightful, not to the sight only, but to every
one of the senses.   Instead of only some yards of snow and fog, I beheld,
suddenly and at one view, a long range of mountain steps, clothed with vegetation, partly of the dark evergreen, partly of the bright green of the spring;
and winding through those wooded hills, the narrow vale of Palerma, with

its clear stream and brilliant gardens; and beyond these, Genoa the Magnificent, with her light-honse, domes, and marble palaces, glittering in the sun; and last, the Mediterranean itself, rising, apparently to me who looked down upon it, into a huge bank of blue, which formed the background of the picture. Was not this a sight for eyes just thawed? Instead of a cold, damp, motionless atmosphere, I breathed highly rarefied air, and felt the soft breeze pass over my face. I listened, doubting; but it was true—the music of the chestnut groves had begun. Presently there were violets by the roadside; and at Campo Marone, the first post town on the sunny side of the Apennines, I received strawberries from a group of girls with bare arms and necks, and fresh flowers in their hair. I was mad with animal joy. Even my English servant (the same who is now an Australian aristocrat) felt the genial change. Though morosely glum by nature, he played some monkey's tricks, ogling the strawberry girls and pulling the postilions tails before my face. And, though anything but a beauty, his stubborn features expanded with happiness, which makes every animal comely after its kind. In the very act of admiring him, I discovered why the Genoese are as lovely as the Alexandrians are frightful. I knew before that Alexandria is placed in a swamp between the Alps and the Apennines; that, consequently, its inhabitants are frozen in winter and stifled in summer; and that at Genoa, the air, never very cold or very hot, always circulates freely; and I had imagined that this great difference of soil and climate must cause the great difference of person. But I still wanted to know the process by which soil and climate deform or beautify the human creature; and it was this that I learned by observing the friskiness of my valet. The Alexandrians suffer from their birth many inconveniences, restraints, and even torments, which the Genoese escape. They feel, therefore, a greater quantity of pain; or, in other words, the Genoese enjoy more happiness. If the face is the mirror of the mind, the whole form may be an index of the habits. Happiness includes animal liberty, and misery includes restraint. Whatever be human society, a face of joy and a form of ease make the perfection of beauty; whilst general deformity is the type of suffering and constraint. As we feel and act continually, so shall we appear. Thus, after all, soil and climate may produce beauty or ugliness by a moral rather than a physical process. What think you of my invention? Apply it to the Australian girls. If you should find in it a reason for their loveliness, I shall not have digressed. Would that all men might adopt the theory; as, in that case, every admirer of beauty must be a warm philanthropist!"

1830.—A Manual of Plain Directions for planting and cultivating Vineyards, and for making Wine, in New South Wales. By James Busby. Sydney. 8vo., 100 pages.

This work is said to have been successful, and to have led to the cultivation of the vine by many colonists.

1833.—Journal of a Tour through some of the Vineyards of Spain and France. By James Busby, Esq. Sydney. 8vo., 140 pages.

Mr. Busby was apparently indefatigable in his labours for the purpose of introducing vine-growing into this Colony. In this, however, he proved to be some quarter of a century before his age. His efforts were not attended with success, although, at the present time, the vineyards of New South Wales have attained to considerable importance in the commercial interests of the country. In the introduction to his "Manual," the following passage is worth extraction :—

"Had New South Wales been settled by a Colony from France, or any other country whose climate is favourable to the growth of the vine, we should at this day have seen few corn-fields without their neighbouring vine-yards ; but the settlers of New South Wales, reared in a country where the vine does not flourish, and where the place of wine is supplied by malt liquors and ardent spirits, have brought with them to the Colony their pre-judice in favour of these liquors, which they continue to use as at Home, forgetting that even in cold countries they form but a poor substitute for wine, and that their pernicious effects are increased tenfold by the heat of such a climate as this."

1833.—Emigration, *considered chiefly in reference to the practi-cability and expediency of importing and settling throughout the territory of New South Wales, a numerous, industrious, and virtuous Agricultural Population.* By J. D. Lang, D.D. Sydney.

1836.—Lectures on Landscape Gardening in Australia. By the late Mr. Thomas Shepherd, of the Darling Nursery; author of "Lectures on the Horticulture of Australia." Sydney. 8vo., 95 pages.

1837.—The Picture of Sydney, and Stranger's Guide in New South Wales. Sydney.

1837.—The Felonry of New South Wales; *being a faithful picture of the Real Romance of Life in Botany Bay, with Anecdotes of Botany Bay Society, and a Plan of Sydney.* By Jas. Mudie, Esq., of Castle Forbes, and late a Magistrate for the Territory of New South Wales. London. 8vo., 362 pages.

The "faithful picture" promised in the title-page of this book is largely disfigured by personalities, aroused by the bitter controversies in which the author had been engaged in the Colony. The book itself is interesting, and deserves reading for the light it throws upon the social life of the period. In Judge Therry's *Reminiscences*, it is said that Mr. Mudie did not venture to publish his work, on account of the libels which crowded its pages. It was privately distributed, and procured for its author a horsewhipping. This was followed by an action for assault and battery, the proceedings at which excited great interest in Sydney, and were published in the form of a pamphlet. Mr. Mudie was distinguished by the barbarous severity with which he treated the unfortunate convicts committed to his care. He appears to have been anything but popular among his fellow colonists.

1837.—Transportation and Colonisation; *or the causes of the comparative failure of the Transportation System in the Australian Colonies; with suggestions for ensuring its future efficiency in subserviency to extensive colonisation.* By J. D. Lang, D.D. London. 8vo., 244 pages.

In this work Dr. Lang entered into a full exposition of the various features of the transportation system, as carried out in this Colony. There is abundant proof here of the really practical character of his intellect—a character which has been too often denied to it. Had his suggestions been attended to, with reference to the subject of Transportation, the Colony would have benefited largely by them. He gives an amusing instance of the absurd manner in which convict labour was sometimes employed. Instead of setting them to work on roads and farms, a party of convicts was once ordered to dig two large pits, and to fill one up with the earth cast out of the other. It is difficult to believe that so absurd a system could ever have existed. With so much labour available for the purposes of settlement, one would think that no time would have been lost in turning it to a practical account.

1837.—A LETTER *to the Right Honorable Lord Viscount Glenelg, Her Majesty's Secretary of State for the Colonies.* By John Bingle, of Puen-Buen, New South Wales; with Documentary Evidence. London. 8vo.

An Appeal from the Local to the Imperial Government, on the ground of some injustice experienced by the writer. He endeavoured to prove that he had been made the victim of political animosity on the part of the former; that he had been deprived of his commission as a Magistrate, subjected to an unfounded charge of cattle-stealing, and otherwise ill-used, for no other reason than the having excited the displeasure of the Governor. One point in the case, on which much stress was laid by the cotemporary Press, was this,—that the indictment against Mr. Bingle had been filed by the Attorney General, who was not only the Crown Prosecutor, but the Grand Jury of the country as well—an amalgamation of functions which is characterized as "a highly unconstitutional anomaly." It is stated also, that the alleged injustice in this case was owing to this combination of political and administrative power in the same functionary.

1837.—New South Wales; its present State and future Prospects. *Being a Statement, with Documentary Evidence, submitted in support of Petitions to Her Majesty and Parliament.* By James Macarthur. London. 8vo.

The author was a son of Mr. John Macarthur, whose name is famous in the land as the introducer of wool-growing. The contents of the work are devoted to an exposition of the various evils, political and social, under which the Colony was labouring: a subject with which the author was fully competent to deal.

1838.—Essays. By James Martin, Esq. Sydney.

A collection of meditations on such subjects as " The Sublime in Nature," " The Thunder Storm," " Botany Bay," " The Colosseum," " Genius," " Pseudo Poets," &c. The author was very young at the time of publication, and is now Prime Minister. The style is rather better than the average of boyish compositions.

1838.—Miscellanies in Prose and Verse. Sydney. 12mo, 144 pages.

The author of this production was Mr. William Woolls. It displays very little power of original thinking. An essay on " the Press" contains the following criticism of colonial journalism in 1838 :—

" I cannot but remark that it is an extraordinary feature in the history of the Colony to find that so many periodicals are in course of circulation. The Press of New South Wales has kept pace with its other improvements ; and now, instead of a single *Government Gazette*, published by authority, and almost devoid of interest, we have no less than seven well printed journals. From time to time a considerable degree of ability has been displayed in the leading articles of the different papers ; and although it is to be lamented that they have, on certain occasions, indulged in much acrimony and invective, it cannot be denied that they have introduced to public notice many useful and important facts, and very materially improved the moral and political condition of our rising Colony."

1839.—New Zealand in 1839. Four Letters to Lord Durham, on the Colonization of that Island, and on the present condition and prospects of its Native Inhabitants. By the Rev. Dr. Lang. London. 8vo., 120 pages.

Quoted in the Encyclopædia Britannica, vol. 21., art. " New Zealand."

1840.—The State of Religion and Education in New South Wales. By W. W. Burton, Esq., one of the Judges of the Supreme Court of that Colony. London.

1840.—Arnoldo and Clara ; *an historical Poem, translated from the Italian of Silvio Pellico.* By W. A. Duncan. Sydney. 12mo., 16 pages.

The translation is in prose.

1840.—A Reply to Judge Burton, of the Supreme Court of New South Wales, *on the state of Religion in the Colony.* By W. Ullathorne, D.D. Sydney. 8vo., 98 pages.

1842.—Female Emigration *considered, in a brief account of the Sydney Emigrants' Home.* By the Secretary. Sydney.

This was the production of Mrs. Chisholm, one of the most practical and self-sacrificing philanthropists of the present age. Her name will not readily be forgotten in this Colony. The little work mentioned above is described in Sidney's *Australian Colonies,* as " a collection of notes and memoranda, interspersed with pithy remarks, and pathetic and comic sketches from real life—a valuable contribution to the art of colonization, and a literary curiosity."

In 1845, Mrs. Chisholm published a " Prospectus of a work to be entitled ' Voluntary Information from the People of New South Wales, respecting the social condition of the middle and working classes in the Colony,' with the view of furnishing the labourer, the mechanic, and the capitalist, with trustworthy information, and pointing out obstructions to emigration that ought to be eradicated."

Mrs. Chisholm's services to the Colony have recently been rewarded by a grant of £500 from the public Treasury.

1843.—OBSERVATIONS ON THE POETICS OF ARISTOTLE, *by Meta-stasio; rendered into English, with a biographical notice of the Author.* Sydney.

The author quotes in his introduction, a passage from a letter of Sir James Macintosh, in which he speaks of Metastasio's Observations as " one of the most ingenious and philosophical pieces of criticism I ever read. It has more good sense and novelty in the Unities than are to be met with anywhere else within the compass of my reading. I wonder it has not been translated." The translation was printed for private distribution, and reviewed in the first number of the *New South Wales Magazine* of 1843. The reviewer said—

" A production of this kind from the Australian press is indeed a novelty, and, from its classical character, can hardly be expected to excite the attention it deserves. That it has been printed at all, however, is a compliment to our tastes, which demands at least the courtesy of acknowledgment."

1843.—MERRY FREAKS IN TROUBLOUS TIMES ; an Historical Operatic Drama, in five Acts. By Charles Nagel, Esq. The music by I. Nathan. Sydney and London.

Mr. Nagel afterwards published another production of this kind. He does not seem to have possessed much merit as a writer.

1843.—PSELLUS' DIALOGUE ON THE OPERATION OF DEMONS. Translated from the Greek, by Marcus Collison. Sydney.

1844.—SYDNEY ILLUSTRATED, *by J. S. Prout ; with letter-press description by John Rae, M.A.* Sydney.

1844.—THE AUSTRALIAN CLASSICAL TEXT BOOK ; *containing the first two books of Eutropius' Roman History, with select Biographies from Cornelius Nepos, and Extracts from Ovid, adapted for the use of the Australian scholar ; with Notes and Examination Questions.* Compiled by T. H. Braim, Esq., of St. John's College, Cambridge, and Head Master of the Sydney College. Sydney.

1845.—A SKETCH OF NEW SOUTH WALES. By J. O. Balfour, Esq., *for six years a Settler in the Bathurst District.* London.

1846.—REMINISCENCES OF AUSTRALIA, *with hints on the Squatter's Life.* By C. P. Hodgson. London.

1847.—PHILLIPSLAND, *or the Country hitherto designated Port Phillip ; its present condition and prospects as a highly eligible field for Emigration.* By J. D. Lang, A.M., Senior Minister of the Presbyterian Church, and Member of the Legislative Council of New South Wales ; Honorary Vice-President of the African Institute of France, and Honorary Member of the Literary Institute of Olinda in the Brazils. Edinburgh. 8vo.

Dr. Lang's ideas as to the nomenclature of these Colonies are founded on common sense, but they have not met with much acceptance. " Phillipsland" is now called Victoria. A vast amount of information is contained in this work ; everything, in fact, at all likely to attract the attention of emigrants is abundantly noted. An address is prefixed to "The Worshipful Company of Publishers in Great Britain and Ireland," in which the author gives his reasons for publishing at his own risk. He says he had " ascertained from two of your number in the British metropolis, and from at least as many in Edinburgh, that our unfortunate Colony of New South Wales had sunk so low in public estimation in this country, under the protracted tyranny of its late Governor, Sir George Gipps, that none of you would venture even to publish a book about it."

1847.—COOKSLAND IN NORTH-EASTERN AUSTRALIA, THE FUTURE COTTON FIELD OF GREAT BRITAIN; *its characteristics, and capabilities for European Colonisation, with a disquisition on the origin, manners, and customs of the Aborigines.* By J. D. Lang, A.M. London.

The object of this work—it may be properly styled a compilation—was to point out the advantages of the north-eastern part of the Colony as a field for emigration. The author did not succeed in fixing the name of "Cooksland" to that part of the country. It is now called Queensland. There is, of course, a large amount of information with regard to the character and capabilities of the country. Not the least valuable portion of the Doctor's writings is the chapter on the Aborigines.

1848.—SYDNEY IN 1848; *illustrated by copper-plate engravings, from drawings by J. Fowles.*

Appeared in fortnightly numbers, the whole comprising forty issues. The plates were accompanied with descriptive letter-press.

1848.—LETTERS ON EDUCATION; *addressed to a Friend in the Bush of Australia.* By Hannah Villiers Boyd. Sydney.

The authoress apparently based her ideas of education on her knowledge of phrenology. "The style of the letters," says a cotemporary reviewer, "is lively and agreeable, and the remarks and particulars interesting and instructive; but there is no systematic course of instruction pointed out or recommended, and the details are desultory and unconnected."

1848.—OBSERVATIONS ON CONVICT AND FREE LABOUR FOR NEW SOUTH WALES. By R. P. Welch, M.R.C.S. (Reprinted from the *Colonial Magazine* for July, 1847.) Sydney.

1848.—EINE DEUTSCHE COLONIE IN STILLEN OCEAN. *Adresse an die ehrenw. Mitglieder des Deutschen Parlaments in Frankfurt und die Deutschen insgesammt.* Von J. D. Lang, Dr. Theol. & Phil. Aus dem Englischen übersezt. Leipsic. 8vo., 45 pages.

Another instance of Dr. Lang's indefatigable efforts to promote emigration to this part of the world. He urged the establishment of a Colony in New Caledonia by Germans. His recommendation was not adopted, but his pamphlet was very favourably noticed in the German account of "The Voyage of the Novara"—a magnificent work recently published by the Austrian Government.

1849.—NOTES ON THE CULTIVATION OF THE VINE AND THE OLIVE, AND ON THE METHODS OF MAKING WINE AND OIL, &c. &c., IN THE SOUTHERN PARTS OF SPAIN, *taken during a tour through Andalusia, in September and October*, 1847. By Lieut.-Col. Sir T. L. Mitchell. Sydney. 4to., 37 pages.

A preface informs us that this work was published by the " Botanic and Horticultural Society," as the first number of their Transactions. It contains a large number of engravings, and as a practical work must be of considerable value.

1849.—LETTERS TO CHARLES BULLER, JUNIOR, ESQ., M.P., from the Australian Patriotic Association. By William Bland. Sydney. 8vo., 238 pages.

[No date.]—THE SOUTHERN EUPHROSYNE AND AUSTRALIAN MISCELLANY, containing Oriental moral tales, original anecdotes, poetry, and music, an historical sketch, with examples of the native aboriginal melodies put into modern rhythm, and harmonized as solos, quartetts, &c ; together with several other original vocal pieces, arranged to a pianoforte accompaniment, by the editor and sole proprietor, I. Nathan, author of *The Hebrew*

Melodies, The Musurgia Vocalis, the successful music in *Sweet-hearts and Wives, The Illustrious Stranger, The King's Fool,* &c., &c. London and Sydney. 4to., 168 pages.

Mr. Nathan was an eccentric gentleman, who possessed considerable talent for music. He was the "Sunburn Nathan!" of Byron's *Hebrew Melodies.* He published many pieces of music in this Colony, and also *A Series of Lectures on the Theory and Practice of Music.* His death took place a year or two ago, after a very lengthened residence in the Colony.

1850.—THE USES AND ABUSES OF TOBACCO. By Dr. F. Campbell.

Dr. Campbell has for many years past conducted the Lunatic Asylum at Tarban Creek. His researches have extended into other fields besides those of mental derangement, and are profusely illustrated by quotations from classical and old English authors.

1851.—NOTES ON THE LATENT RESOURCES OF POLYNESIA. By Charles St. Julian. Sydney. 12mo.

Mr. St. Julian is Law Reporter to the *Herald.* He resided for some years in the Islands previous to his arrival in Sydney.

1852.—FREEDOM AND INDEPENDENCE FOR THE GOLDEN LANDS OF AUSTRALIA; THE RIGHT OF THE COLONIES, AND THE INTEREST OF BRITAIN AND OF THE WORLD. By J. D. Lang, D.D., A.M. London. 8vo., 334 pages.

The *Westminster Review* spoke of this work as follows :—

"With the preceding work (his 'History of New South Wales') Dr. Lang issued another, bearing the startling title of ' Freedom and Independence for the Golden Lands of Australia,' in which he partitions Eastern Australia into seven provinces (three of them being created and baptised by himself), which are to constitute a Federal Republic ; and, as if this were already settled, a map is prefixed, altered to suit the new state of things, and, with its coloured divisions, presenting so much the respectable appearance of a *fait accompli,* as somewhat to prepossess the reader in favour of the work.

o

Nor will he be disappointed with it ; for, contrary to what might be expected, it contains much calm, elaborate reasoning, supported by abundance of historical and legal references ; but after all, the question is not,—Are the Australian Colonies entitled to Independence? but,—Are they prepared for it?"

1853.—NATIONAL EDUCATION. Melbourne. 8vo., 365 pages.

The author's name is G. W. Rusden, an Inspector of Schools under the Board of National Education in this Colony.

1853.—THE PRODUCTIONS, INDUSTRY, AND RESOURCES OF NEW SOUTH WALES. By Charles St. Julian, and E. K. Silvester. Sydney, 12mo.

The contents of this volume originally appeared in the *Herald,* with which journal the authors were connected as reporters.

1854.—SYDNEY REVELS OF BACCHUS, CUPID, AND MOMUS ; *being choice and humourous selections from Scenes at the Sydney Police Office and other public places, during the last three years.* By C. A. Corbyn, Newspaper Reporter. Dedicated, by permission, to G. R. Nichols, Esq., M.L.C., by his obliged and faithful servant, the Author. Sydney. 8vo., 136 pages.

1856.—THE AUSTRALIAN MUSICAL ALBUM. Sydney. 4to.

A handsomely printed collection of music, composed in Sydney, with a preface by Mr. Fowler. Musical publications, it may be added, are extremely common in Sydney.

1857.—AUSTRALIAN ESSAYS ON SUBJECTS POLITICAL, MORAL, AND RELIGIOUS. By James Norton, Esq., senior, of Elswick, in the County of Cumberland New South Wales, Member of the Legislative Council of New South Wales. London. 4to., 136 pages.

1857.—AUSTRALIA AS IT REALLY IS, IN ITS LIFE, SCENERY, AND ADVENTURE : *with the character, habits, and customs of its Aboriginal Inhabitants, and the prospects and extent of its Gold Fields.* By F. Eldershaw. London. 8vo., 270 pages.

The author is a Clerk in the Legislative Assembly.

1858.—PETER 'POSSUM'S PORTFOLIO. Sydney. 8vo. 220 pages.

A collection of various pieces in prose and verse, contributed to different periodicals. It contains some remarkably good writing. The author, Mr. Rowe, was associated with Mr. Fowler in carrying on the "Month," and in that magazine appeared most of the articles republished in the "Portfolio." First comes a short tale, called "Arthur Owen, an Autobiography," narrating the experiences of a hunchback; then some prose sketches of life and manners, graphically written, and very amusing; and, lastly, a series of verses, most of which are translations from the Greek, Latin, and German. Mr. Rowe is evidently a fine scholar, as well as a brilliant magazine writer. It is painful to thiuk that his career in this Colony was not so successful as it ought to have been, and that his "Portfolio" was published for the purpose, as stated in the preface, of relieving his necessities.

1860.—HOW I BECAME ATTORNEY GENERAL OF NEW BARATARIA. An experiment at treating facts in the forms of fiction. Originally published in *The Southern Cross* weekly journal. Sydney. 8vo., 24 pages.

The authorship of this brilliant satire has been alluded to in the article on the *Southern Cross*.

1861.—QUEENSLAND, AUSTRALIA; *a highly eligible field for Emigration, and the future Cotton Field of Great Britain; with a Disquisition on the origin, manners, and customs of the Aborigines.* By J. D. Lang, D.D., A.M., &c., &c. London. 8vo., 445 pages.

This seems to be an enlarged edition of the author's previous work on Cooksland. It is of much the same character, abounding in practical information, particularly with reference to the capabilities of Queensland for the growth of cotton.

1863.—LOST, BUT NOT FOR EVER; *my personal Narrative of Starvation and Providence in the Australian Mountain Regions.* By the Rev. R. W. Vanderkiste, Author of "The Dens of London." London. 8vo., 357 pages.

[No date.]—POLITICAL PORTRAITS of some of the Members of the Parliament of New South Wales, including Cowper, Hay, Robertson, Martin, Forster, Wilson, Arnold, Piddington, Dr. Lang, Hoskins, Dalley, Dalgleish. By David Buchanan, Esq. (late M.P. for Morpeth). Price, 1s. Sydney. 8vo., 56 pages.

Published about the year 1863.

1864.—LECTURES DELIVERED IN AUSTRALIA. By John Woolley, D.C.L. London. 8vo.

The subjects of these lectures are principally of an ethical character—a branch of study to which the author was extremely partial. The lectures were nearly all delivered at Schools of Arts. Dr. Woolley was the finest scholar we have ever seen in the Colony, and many proofs both of taste and learning may be found in this volume.

The *Westminster Review* spoke of it as follows :—" *Lectures delivered in Australia* is a title sufficient in itself to create interest, and few can glance over the subjects discussed in this volume without some impulse of curiosity to know how social questions of the greatest importance present themselves at the antipodes to an English Professor ; and such curiosity will give place to admiration and thankfulness for the enlightened spirit and earnestness of tone which pervade these pages. Three of the lectures are inaugural addresses delivered at the opening of the University of Sydney, in October, 1852, at the Sydney School of Arts in 1856, and an introductory discourse at the same in 1857. They one and all bear the stamp of eloquence which springs from the union of a deep reverential love of the beautiful and the true with the hearty living sympathy of practical philanthrophy, and seem to express the vigour and exhilaration inspired by a fresh start in a new sphere, which, how great soever may be its dangers and difficulties, is unfettered by some of the intellectual bonds which press most heavily upon ourselves."

1864.—A Treatise on the Cultivation of Flax and Hemp. By Francis Campbell, M.D. Third edition. Sydney. 8vo., 80 pages.

1864.—Scab in Sheep, and its Cure. By Alexander Bruce. Sydney. 8vo.

1865.—Under the Holly.—A Cantata. Words by R. P. Whitworth ; Music by J. C. Fisher. Sydney.

1866.—A Handbook of plain and practical Directions for Sugar-cane planting, Sugar-making, and the Distillation of Rum. By F. A. Bell. Sydney.

1866.—Rural Architecture. By Harold Brees. Sydney.

A large number of Pamphlets, Book Almanacs, Directories, and similar publications, may be found in our public libraries. It is not thought necessary to mention any, except a few Pamphlets rendered important by the subjects of which they treat.

Sydney : Thomas Richards, Government Printer.—1866.

www.ingramcontent.com/pod-product-compliance
Lightning Source LLC
Chambersburg PA
CBHW030546040726
47497CB00008B/2602